DEDICATION

For my brother Harry
Open each day as if it were a precious gift!

Away in Irma's Manger
By Mike Burke

Frist Edition, 2018

Cover and Interior Design: Madelein Puche & Deborah Rockholt

Cover Imagen: © Wycon Cosmetics

Printed in the United States of America

FORWARD

"Away in Irma's Manger" is a work of adult humor fiction based on the many fanciful stories I contrived over twenty years. Thanks to the urging of my wife Sherri and my cousin Beth Creed I figuratively took pen in hand. I am approaching my eightieth year and have hopefully preserved these adventures for my family and friends.

Thanks to the technical and editorial support of my gracious friends Mike Britt and most especially Deb Rockholt without whom I would have never completed the book.

I trust that no one shall be offended as it was all written in jest, and those who know me are keenly aware of what my jest is worth.

Mike Burke   April 15, 2018

FARTICUS

Mikey opened his eyes and quietly slid out of bed as to not wake Sherri. It was coming up on 7 am. He had gotten up early for his whole life and Sherri could stay in bed forever. The dog stirred at the foot of the bed, but immediately fell back into dog oblivion as there was no sensed danger.

Down the stairs of the neat little beach townhouse Mikey hit the coffee button, squared himself away and slid on his beach shorts and flip flops. He always wore a fresh decent shirt to keep him from being mistaken for a poor homeless fellow, which was possible at his age in the early morning hours in Cocoa Beach. Out in the slightly worn SUV, coffee in hand he rolled out of the complex and in five minutes was parked at the beach itself on Slater Way.

Slater Way was named for Cocoa Beach's deservedly world famous professional surfer Kelly Slater who had won the world championship eleven times, and who was also honored with a fine statue two blocks away.

The entrance over the sand dune was railed with mooring line artfully cascaded on paired four foot high dock piles leading to the beach and ocean. A natural group of windblown trees formed an arch over the entrance giving the feeling of arrival at a very special place.

There were many weddings held on the beach as the archway allowed the silhouette of the bride to be perfectly framed as she proceeded to her nuptials perhaps thirty yards to the sand. There was no standard or required dress. Anything from shorts to full formal wear. On several occasions Mikey respectfully waited as the windblown veils and trains filled the entrance with a heavenly light.

"A perfect picture for their special day," he would reflect.

Today there were no weddings. Mikey opened the back of the SUV, stretched and had a final gulp of coffee. He then took his five gallon blue plastic bucket and a three foot long trash grabber out of the vehicle and was ready for this morning's mission of cleaning the beach and saving the mermaids. Mikey was a short person by any standard. He claimed five foot six, but the years had shrunk and worn him down a few more inches. Vertically challenged like Napoleon as he would say.

The sand was still cool so he hooked his flip flops to his belt and started picking up the trash as he worked his way towards the water.

"Ahhh, it must be Monday", he muttered to himself as he grabbed a used diaper, food wrappers and remnants of a dumped ashtray from a vacated parking slot. "The Orlando crowd was here with the kids."

For the next hour Mikey worked his way south down the beach filling his bucket several times with an array of plastic bottles, hundreds of cigarette butts, glass bottles and discards of all colors and then dumping the trash in the larger buckets positioned on the beach. Sherri had painted 'Mikey's Bucket List' in silver on the bucket. There was a sticker that said "Clean the Earth, It's not your Uranus". Bumper stickers from Cocoa Beach, Key Largo, Outer Banks, and Key West were arrayed on the side as was the sticker from his daughter Rebecca and her husband's "Wake-and-Bakery" coffee shop in Glacier, Washington.

The stated bucket list painted on the side was:

1. Clean the Beach

2. Feed the Mermaids

The early morning crowd had mostly arrived. Paddle boarders and surfers, older tourists, daily walkers and joggers as well as a couple of families dragging the kids and all their gear across the sand. One rarely saw a dog as animals were not allowed on the beaches of Brevard County, which had its good and bad points. The good point being that one hardly stepped on a poop. Having completed his collection Mikey took a turn and headed off the sand to the main drag where the bars and cafes lined Minutemen Causeway.

The VFW was just down the street and was his usual final morning stop where he helped Charley the day man get things going. He was a retired butcher and Mikey's good friend.

"Yo Mikey," said Charley, "how's it hanging?"

"You talkin' to me?" Mikey replied in his best native Jersey accent. "Got some coffee?"

The VFW was one of the oldest buildings in Cocoa Beach. It recently had added a new outside porch to accommodate smokers who had been banned inside the small bar. Most of the downtown was in the final stages of upgrading, but had managed to retain much of the old beach charm. The early Space and Shuttle era was being replaced by a new breed of Rocketeers at Kennedy Space Center about eight miles up the road. It was still a thrill when Mikey saw the launches and now the recoveries, "just like Flash Gordon", he would say. "I wonder whatever happened to Ming the Merciless?"

After a couple of shared silent gulps Charley relaxed into a chair and smiled, "This is a good place to watch the girls."

"Yeah, and now that I am not even a senior, but friggin ELDERLY, I still love watching the mermaids", Mikey replied.

"Mikey, I always wanted to ask you how you got started in this picking' up trash and feeding the mermaids stuff?"

Mikey took another sip of his coffee and started his tale.

"Well it has been something under development for quite a while, but about ten years ago I finally got to go to Ireland. It was a tour sort of thing and Sherri didn't want to go because there was no smoking for about twenty hours from the time you got on the plane in Orlando, transferred to another in Newark and then across the Atlantic ocean to Shannon Airport which is non-smoking, and then on a non-smoking bus to the non-smoking hotel. AND she didn't like Guinness, only American brewskis, so I went alone. It was something that was on the top of my Bucket List."

"The first day after we landed at Shannon, I slept in an ancient castle after visiting Dirty Nellie's Bar. So the next day or maybe the third day our tour made a stop in Killarney where we were free to roam about. I decided to visit the local St Mary's Church, to light a candle for all of the Burkes, Flynns, Traceys, Plunketts and Fitzsimmons who never made it back. In front of the church is a huge tree which marks the graves of many, many children who died during the starvation. There was a mass at the main altar so I found an out of the way little side altar and lit my candles. Sitting down I looked up to the smiling face of Saint Teresa and under the statue was inscribed her mantra,

"I will live my Heaven by doing good on Earth."

What a wonderful thing I thought, and I can really say it was a small miracle which instilled me with trying to do good, like cleaning up the beach to remember the children buried there and to try to preserve our beach for future generations."

Charley said, "That was very moving, very nice."

Mikey smiled. "Ah but the next day I found out a much more revealing thing about my family when I discovered the legend of my ancient Italian ancestor Burkus Giganticus Padorkus, who was also known as Farticus Burkus."

"Wait, just wait a minute," Charley said in a slightly raised voice," I thought you were in Ireland?"

"I was, I was, let me explain please," Mikey replied.

"In the port town of Cobh, I went to one of these ancestry tracer places. Cobh was the last port of departure for the Titanic on its fateful voyage, and also the departure port for hundreds of thousands of Irish immigrants during the Great Starvation. The Trail of Tears marks the path they took to the ships, most never to see their families and friends ever again. An elderly gentleman who looked and perhaps smelled about 150 years old, and who was lightly pickled in Guinness that day, took my family information and turned away from his desk while summoning the sweetest young smiling miss named Meghan Tracey from the back room. She had long dark hair and very fair skin which was a shade darker than the pure white skin of most Irish. Meghan greeted me with a sweet polite smile and warmly welcomed me as she began her search on her laptop. After what seemed about ten minutes, she smiled knowingly, looked me in the eye and said, "I think we are related, because I am one of the Black Irish as you can see". Then she told me the story of how many of the Irish got black hair:

THE LEGEND OF FARTICUS BURKUS

About 125 AD back in Rome itself, my ancient ancestor Burkus Giganticus Padorkus was born to the family of a Roman General. He was named Giganticus Padorkis at birth because he had the largest male organ ever seen by the midwife, who actually fainted when he came forth. Giganticus Padorkus grew up to be a soldier like his father and was known as a great builder of public baths which were everywhere for wealthy and average citizens too. So he had a lot of side jobs that were under the table sort of speak. Now, when Burkus Giganticus Padorkus was finished with a bath, he would sit half naked on the bottom of the bath and flatulate, producing bubbles to test the resonance of the marble.

"Now if the bubbles that came to the surface and made this noise...BURKE, pause, BURKE", it met the stamp of approval for clarity, resonance and circulation."

"Burke was of course translated to Latin and became BURKUS, hence the name Burkus Giganticas Padorkus. It is believed that

eventually he was also known as Farticus
Burkus."

Mikey paused for another sip of his coffee.
Charley sucked down some beer.

"Well, here is how Farticus Burkus got to
Ireland. One day he was finishing a bath in
Rome for a wealthy Senator's villa when he
met and fell for their daughter, Lotsa
Felationis. She was very lovely and their
passionate courtship was nothing but
Padorkus and Felationis. In a short while they
were married, but alas there was no more
felationis but still a lot of padorkus. In due
course twins, a boy and a girl, were born, with
the boy named Less and the girl named Lessa.
This resulted in no more felationis and Less
and Lessa Padorkus. A terrible problem for a
young Roman Legionnaire."

Charley said, "I know the feeling".

Mikey continued his story once again.

"As fate would have it the Emperor Hadrian
had invaded England, and decided to build a
wall across the entire country to keep the
barbarians to the north. Farticus Burkus and

his legion were sent to Britain to help build the wall, and Burkus was assigned to be in charge of building a bath at each garrison along the wall. Burkus said farewell to his little family and headed out to do his duty. The baths were built rapidly and were the pride of the legion. Every bath received and passed the Farticus Burkus test. This in the period he was nicknamed Farticus.   One day Burkus was informed by his centurion that Hadrian himself would be in England in three weeks to inspect the wall and had ordered a special bath for himself and his entourage. Burkus excitedly took to the task and was nearing completion when suddenly the General himself said, "You must hurry Burkus.   Hadrian will be here tomorrow."

The men worked all night and as the sun rose all was in readiness EXCEPT the final testing. Burkus lowered himself into the bath, took a deep breath, and red in the face POOPED IN THE EMPORER'S BATH."

The legionnaires all began yelling "Poopus, Poopus Giganticus" except Burkus's assistant Charmin, who exclaimed,

"Run Burkus run, take my horse, the Emperor's guard will chop off your padorkus", and Burkus quickly mounted the gallant steed and rode into the forest before the unforgivable offense was seen by the Emperor. He would never again be able to return to Rome.

Away and away he rode to the shores of the sea, where he purchased a small boat and pushed off the shore into a gloomy storm. Fortunately, the little boat had a sail and after three days Burkus grounded on a beach in what today is Ireland. Exhausted and starving he crawled onto the rocks and fell into a deep sleep."

At this point Mikey could see that Charley needed another beer and the story still had a little way to go.

"You know Charley as I said the young lady at the ancestry place was named Meghan Tracey. Very pretty and very kind. But I kept staring at her because she resembled my father's cousin, Diane Fitzsimmons."

Charley smiled, "How kind?"

"Oh no, no fooling around, Sherri would brain me"

"Is that the end of the story?" Charley asked.

"Oh no, " said Mikey, "It gets better."

"As the sun broke through an overcast sky a beautiful young woman with long dark hair came wandering down the beach searching for clams and such. She was known in these parts as Wild Nellie, but there were rumors that Wild Nellie was really a mermaid who had shed her mermaid skin and came to live ashore with the humans. She lived simply by herself in a cottage by the ocean. Suddenly she came upon Burkus sleeping in the sand, and was impassioned by his handsome face and muscular body as well as large endowment. She helped Burkus to her cottage and said, "Would you care for some breakfast?" Well, it wasn't long before they were passionately in love. They lived happily together for about thirty years and had twelve children, all of whom had black hair, according to Meghan at the ancestry search."

People walking by the cottage in the evening would hear their love making as Wild Nellie would cry out, "My, Oh My, Oh" which became so well known in Ireland that a whole county was named for her, County Mayo. So this why I try to do good like Saint Teresa, and it is also the reason that I take care of the mermaids who are descended from my ancestor Wild Nellie and finally that is why when my Italian friends greet me on Columbus Day with "Napalitano", "Calabrese", "Sicigliano" to identify their particular Italian ancestry, I always exclaim "Mayonaisea" in honor of Wild Nellie of County Mayo, the mother of the Irish with black hair."

Charley was speechless, so Mikey put down his coffee and headed for the door and home. "See ya tomorrow Charley."

"See ya tomorrow Farticus.

THE GRAND BOOMA

Sherri was already up and painting sea shells when Mikey got back from the beach. Their old Westie named Lulu, greeted Mikey with a matter of fact nose rub on his legs and then laid down on the cool kitchen tiles. Sherri and Mikey were sometimes called 'the Odd Couple' behind their back. She was twenty years younger than he, stood five foot ten and was as redneck as a Norfolk, Virginia girl could be. They met in Norfolk when Mikey was sailing as merchant Captain of the USNS Soderman. The ship was docked in Norfolk to crew up and sail for the Indian Ocean and Persian Gulf with military cargo for the US Marines. They first met on the telephone when Sherri worked in the Norfolk crewing hall, a job that required some tough and colorful language. She previously had worked in a shipyard office working closely with the men and woman repairing ships. They all loved her because she really cared for working people and their families. She had never found the right guy and had never married. Mikey on the other hand had divorced twice. What they shared was the maritime business and taking care of their crews.

One cold February night Mikey was at a small Norfolk waterfront bar and restaurant having some of his favorite Filipino pancet. The door suddenly flung open and there stood Sherri in her black leather jacket with 'USA' on its back. The bar was almost entirely filled with patrons, but when Sherri appeared in the door the bar buzz stopped, sort of like Wyatt Earp walking into the Last Chance Saloon.

Sherri strolled over to Mikey's table and, without permission sat down and said, " Hey sailor, you new here in town. Think you're going to get real lucky?"

Mikey for once in his life was speechless.

"Hey," she smiled "you got a twenty I can hold? I want to play some pool and I'm broke". They have been together since that day.

"Those are some beautiful shells that you're doing love. I brought you back a few nice ones that might be suitable for painting."

Sherri had decided to 'give up the grape' four

years previously after a serious warning from her doctor. It was really tough to not be at the beach bars. One lost a lot of social life not to mention bar friends. Real friends still came around, but not as much anymore. About the same time that Sherri gave up the bar scene their annual trip to a rental in the Keys sort of morphed the direction of their recent lives. Mikey was completely overwhelmed by the paper and plastic trash that accumulated daily along the shore in the Keys and started picking it up. At first it was a handful, then a small bag, then a larger bag, and now a five gallon bucket to fill the larger bags. It became a daily habit that he carried back to Cocoa Beach. Soon Sherri started painting shells that he brought home. It replaced a void left by her sobriety. Her art work got better and better, and Mikey started taking the beautifully painted shells to the beach. He would give them out to small children and those expressing their appreciation for his trash work. He also had special ones in his pocket for lovers and newlyweds when he happened upon a beach wedding. He somehow came up with the story that his wife was a mermaid and was in charge of this part of the beach and as ordered by King Neptune through Neptune's Royal Scribe Davy Jones, Mikey was directed to give a pretty shell to the special beach goers with Neptune's message not to leave trash on the beach or throw trash into the ocean. It was as simple as that. He would always add that his mermaid would not make him breakfast if he failed in his mission.

He never approached children or women alone, except if they came to him with trash for his bucket or thank him, as there were so many things happening in the world he might be taken as a fondler or groper.   His daily clean tropical shirts or colorful t-shirts also simplified approaching people who were sometimes suspicious of an older stranger approaching with a shell extended in his hand. The floppy sun protection hat was something of a trademark as well.

"So, did you give away any shells today?" Sherri asked.

"I did," Mikey replied, "there was a nice young couple with a toddler visiting from Germany, I gave them the shell with sunshine and flowers and a palm tree."

He paused, "but I hate to say it was a sad day too, as I helped the city beach lady bag a big loggerhead turtle that came in dead on the last tide. It wasn't too bad as decay hadn't started. The lady, Margie, said it was apparently malnourished, maybe ate too much plastic or Styrofoam. Win a few, lose a few"

Lulu stirred and then flopped back to sleep. Her morning walk and breakfast had tired her.

"You know", started Mikey, "lots of people still don't think that pollution and climate change are for real. So I was thinking that when I was born in 1939, just before World War Two, there were, I think, about one point nine billion people on the planet. Then the war killed off somewhere around one hundred fifty million, but now we are pushing eight billion people worldwide and well over two billion don't have a proper toilet."

"Don't you mean a proper BOOMA?" Sherri interrupted.

"Yes, BOOMA, but in other words there are more people on the planet without a proper toilet than there were on the ENTIRE PLANET at the beginning of my life!!!"

"Well the good news is that your GRAND BOOMA t-shirt just arrived," she said as she handed him the package.

"Anything from the Pope," Mikey smiled.

"Nope, sorry. Hey put the shirt on," she said.

It was a simple white shirt with the words 'GRAND BOOMA' in medium blue letters across his chest. Below that was a blue porta john with 'Booma' inscribed on the door.

"Perfect," said Mikey. "I needed another crusade."

Mikey had spent almost fifty years at sea, both in the Navy and the Merchant Marine. In his travels around the world he had heard and mostly learned of necessity the words for *toilet* ln many different languages.

He often reflected that many travelers, especially Americans, didn't know how to say 'please or thank you or hello' in a foreign language.   When it came to "Where is the toilet" in Japanese or Chinese or Spanish or

Icelandic, the visitor in most cases was really at a loss. The other language problem that really upset him was Americans asking, "Where is the BATHROOM", when they wanted the toilet or ladies room or men's room.

So he hit upon the idea of a simple universal word for toilet that would be the same in every language. The word he chose was BOOMA because it contained a B and an M and an OO and an A for AHHH thus BOOMA!!!

"This will be my contribution to world peace. Everyone can be comfortable when nature calls, and all I want is to be "THE GRAND BOOMA." No matter where you travel everyone will know what a Booma is.

He had a GRAND BOOMA shirt many years ago when the idea first grabbed him. It was black with purple letters, hard to read. So now he wanted something brighter and added the porta john. Mikey had written a letter to Pope Francis with his idea, but no response.

He really had never met Pope Francis but pulled a few gullible legs about their alleged relationship saying that he had met the Pope in Argentina. According to Mikey he suggested to the Pope that his Papal name be Francis, for Francis Albert Sinatra. Then he claimed to have told the Pope that every Sunday his Holiness could stand on the balcony overlooking the thousands gathered below in Saint Peter's Square, open his arms and in five different languages sing "I did it my way".

This story troubled Sherri, "You know some of the things that you say could be very offensive to some people, or just hurt their feelings."

"Well, I have to agree", replied Mikey. "The one that really gets me in trouble is when I suggest that since the Bible says that Jesus is the Son of God, and that Jesus's Mother might be God itself, and that Mary was a brown skinned Middle Eastern woman. Jesus being the son of God, and Mary is his Mother, then perhaps God could be a dark skinned Middle Eastern woman."

"You are going to get yourself killed some day."

"Well, I hope not and I don't try to offend on purpose, just trying to discuss the eternal question of who and what is God and this great universe. I mean just look at the gazillions of stars and planets that have been discovered in the last twenty years by the Hubbell telescope launched right down the street from Cape Canaveral. Yet any way that you cut it there WAS a beginning point or is it beyond our comprehensive ability to understand without a beginning point something that is a person's religion or lack of a formal religion seems to me, is to a great extent, an attempt to understand his or her place in this vast universe, and what is the proper way to spiritually and practically conform to that existence. The practicality being the proper way to conduct one's life which also satisfies the spirituality of their relation with a Force or Power."

Mikey poured a cup of coffee and continued.

"The thing that really upsets me is how different peoples over the ages to this very day actually KILL one another in the name of an all merciful Higher Power. Whenever I try to just discuss different concepts or religions, it seems that people feel that they MUST take a position, which means that it is no longer a discussion but a confrontation."

The conversation was getting pretty heavy and the subject was dropped. Mikey slipped on the Grand Booma T shirt and pushed his thinning dark hair back in place.

"I think we need some milk," he said. "I'll drop by the Dollar store and stir up some Boomas".

CASH FOR CLUNKERS

The Dollar General Store was a place where you usually ran into one or two people that you knew. It had a good selection of food and basics. Its central location didn't require an auto in most cases. The library, post office and hardware store were just next door.

On this particular day Mikey ran into his friend Gustav a lifelong commercial fisherman. His hands were so powerful that Mikey always checked them for barnacles. Gustav was cautious when he met Mikey because of his sometimes outrageous stories. He was a little older than Mikey and like others skeptical about the direction that the country and the world seemed to be going.

Some years earlier the two had a conversation at a beach bench off Slater Way. Gustav's wife had recently died, and he was still sorting things out. He spent many hours looking at the water and evaluating fishing conditions while lingering over old fond memories.

On that day Gustav started talking politics and that was not Mikey's favorite subject, so he began to soften the conversation,

"You know Gustav, did I ever tell you about my job with the Chinese Connection Motor Company."

Gustav looked at Mikey but said nothing. "Yes, I was surprised myself, but somehow the White House got my name when Sherri tried to trade me in under the Cash for Clunkers program."

"She what!!??"

"Yeah, she just wanted to see what would happen, or so she says. So before long this very official type guy calls up and started asking me if I had ever been to China, and I said I had when I was working on my Grand Booma Program."

Gustav smiled and relaxed a bit, "Yeah I remember when you told me about the Grand Booma. How's that going?"

"Well, right now it's on the back burner, but I'm getting a t-shirt made."

Mikey continued, "It turned out the new administration was looking for someone with an imagination and had some experience dealing with the Chinese, so it was a good fit. I had dealt with Chinese port officials several times with no problem.

I told this fellow I had three basic models in mind, the first model would be a fine limousine called The Long Dong. My advertising for that would be centered on a world famous basketball player who would say in the TV ads, I have a Long Dong."

Gustav adjusted his Marlin's baseball hat.

"The next model was a compact called the Little Wee. My TV ad for that would be a Chinese gymnast appearing in her tumbling outfit and saying "I've got a Wee Wee".

Gustav shook his head and said, "You're kidding!"

"Ah, but the best would be an SUV with simulated wood paneling called "The Woodie", and we would have a Chinese golfer or maybe a surfer dude standing next to the car saying "Every time I drive my SUV

I've got a Woodie".

This was a bit too much for Gustav.

"Mikey, how do you find the time to get involved in this? I would just like to be fishing again with my sons or have a nice meal with my wife," which brought a tear to his eye. "What good is all of this?"

Mikey took a chug of cold water and offered some to Gustav.

"No thanks."

"Well, this means we would be building cars for the Chinese instead of them building cars for us. You know, jobs. It's all about jobs and my most revolutionary model would be for the environment, "The Farticus", named after my Roman ancestor Farticus Burkus. The Farticus is still in the developmental stage and will be the subject of a lot of push back, but the Farticus will run on human gas. Initially we will get gas from septic tanks through a new invention, The Reverse Beano Line which Sherri developed while working for a local plumber, with later plans to be able to provide gas directly from the driver, him or herself. This of course will be very controversial and require an outpatient surgery. But if this option is chosen the owner gets a lifetime supply of beans, six choices to pick from."

Gustav again scratched his head but was comfortable with the story. "Why call it the Farticus?

" Well, as I said, I got the name Farticus from my ancient Roman ancestor Padorkus Giganticus who also may have been known as Farticus Burkus. In fact the last time I spoke with my friend Meghan Tracey back in Ireland she informed me that a statue had recently been unearthed in Ireland with the name of Farticus Burkus engraved on its pedestal. There was also a damaged statue with it of a woman with the engraving of Nellius Hornius, but I haven't had time to further investigate. The strange thing about Nellie seems to be that she appears to have been a mermaid."

"A mermaid," exclaimed Gustav, "I think that I saw one once, but it probably was a manatee."

"Now that would be a pretty homely mermaid," replied Mikey.

"I guess so, "said Gustav and his mind began to drift off.

"Well, I have to go now and pick up some trash. I'm expecting a phone call from Shanghai and I left my cell phone in the car. See ya later, Gustav".

Gustav was a very smart old sailor and didn't really believe much of what Mikey said. He quietly smiled when Mikey stopped about fifty yards down the beach and handed out shells to a family of visitors. They appeared to be from India or some far off distant land.

IMAGINE

The world had become a very divisive and angry place since September eleventh. In spite of the bloodshed, pain and trillions of dollars of national treasure being spent over the years, few if any Americans seemed to know much about the Muslims and their religious and personal differences. Many feared or even hated Muslims simply because of the extremists' atrocities.

Mikey would sometimes ask, and usually get into trouble, "What are the differences between a Sunni and a Shia? Are the Taliban, al Qaeda and ISIS Sunni or Shia? Why do they so hate one another and non-Muslims that they blew themselves up by the thousands because of their hate?"

One morning Mikey said to Sherri, "I really can't think of one person that we personally know who would wrap themselves in dynamite and pull the pin. Not one, I know a lot of goofy people, and we all shared the sadness when our friend went down to the beach and checked out with his revolver because he was suffering so much mental pain, and couldn't get an appointment at the VA. I remember the Buddhist monks self-emulating in the middle of the street in Vietnam, but never actually knew a person who believed so fervently that they would go to eternal happiness by killing a bunch of woman and children in the name of God."

"They get extra credit or something like that," replied Sherri. "Other people have done that over time, remember that picture 'Gunga Din' where the Guru jumps into the pit of snakes?"
"That's true, but he didn't take anyone with him."
"Well, why do the Sunni and Shia hate each other?" she asked.

"From what I've read it all actually started around 1400 years ago when Muhammed died and left no male heir. There was a terrible argument amongst his followers and family as to who would be the successor and they split into the Sunni and Shia. Also the two different groups disagreed over the interpretation of the Koran. As a result a lot of respected holy men on both sides were murdered in one way or another and the revenge motives escalated for all these years. At the time of the Protestant Reformation, Christians did similar things, or the Spanish Inquisition which targeted Jewish people."

"Well, there was a lot of politics if you ask me, and I am still confused", Sherri replied. "This is a very tricky subject and you and a lot of your buddies have been involved with it. Those who have lost loved ones are very much like the families who lost family in Vietnam and all the other wars. When you start telling people that you invented the Burka and the Burkini bathing suit you are somewhat oblivious to what some people might say or do or whose feelings you might hurt. Think about it before you start talking."

Mikey pondered her last statement and finally said, "You are very right on that one. Do you remember that fellow Jake?"

"Not really."
"Well, Jake was or is a reserve Navy officer. He got called up at the age of forty and sent to Afghanistan for a year. Think about that!!

Sending a forty year old Jewish tax accountant guy into Kabul. Naval Intelligence. This was about six years ago when things were hot. Jake told me that he was assigned to an office in Kabul where he distributed cold cash to Taliban in an effort to convert them. He said that one guy was a big time opium grower and they gave him five million, I mean five million freekin' dollars cash in a backpack to stop growing opium. They even relocated him and his three wives to the States."

"Where did he go? Did he move to Utah?" interjected Sherri.
"I don't know where he landed," Mikey answered, "but five million could have paid a lot of medical bills someplace."

"What's your point?" Asked Sherri.

"Well, I guess that I ramble on because I am trying to figure out my place in the universe, like most people. And that it really doesn't matter what path one takes but that old axiom, 'to thy own self be true.' If you dare, then you can be comfortable with yourself and your beliefs. That's all. Trying to keep it simple.

When you are on watch on a ship on the bridge, especially at night on a long transit, there is just you and your watch mate cruising along in a perfect sea in perfect weather. The heavens are such a mass of stars and it never escaped me to realize my own insignificance on one hand, and how important the things I did were for the ship and with the crew that depended on my good judgement and knowledge. That was something that I truly miss now that I am beached with age." Then he quoted the Bible:

"They that go down to the sea in ships and do business in great waters; these see the work of the Lord and his wonders in the deep..."
Psalm 107:23-24
There is something else, he continued.

"Many a night I thought after finishing a pleasant bridge watch, I would lay in my bunk and not think of what was in the sky, but what was in the depths beneath the ship. An entire different universe of fishes, whales, dolphins, squids, sharks and such. Maybe even mermaids."

IRMA

If you live in Florida you should expect hurricanes just as if you live in the Colorado Rockies or the Washington Cascades you should expect snow. Mikey had seen a predicted track similar to IRMA when hurricane ANDREW tore Miami apart. He was able to avoid ANDREW by moving his ship out of Port Everglades and take shelter south of Cape San Antonio on the western end of Cuba. Now he wasn't on a ship, but in a house and the early projections had IRMA passing almost directly through Cocoa Beach as MATTHEW had done the previous year.

"I think we should head over to the west coast near Crystal River," he told Sherri. "We should be far enough away in the less dangerous semi-circle over there."

"Well, I have an important check up with the doctor on Tuesday. How soon do we have to go?"

"Not later than Thursday because of the traffic, and because there might be a mandatory evacuation again," said Mikey.

Sherri had her procedure done and then found a not too expensive place near Crystal River on the internet, "Hey, it's scallop season over there, we can make it a mini-vacation", she said.

They left Cocoa Beach and headed to Florida's west coast on Wednesday as things were getting chaotic on the highways and gasoline was getting short. Taking local highways and avoiding the freeways, they made it cross state in four hours, slowed only by jam ups at I-75 near The Villages. A line of huge travel trailers were inching along the right lane to the highway I-75 northbound entrance.

"Look!! There's about 50 pimped up golf carts coming up the shoulder," said Mikey.

The golf cart caravan passed slowly as they proceeded. Many were waving American Flags.

I'll bet they are singing *On the Way to Cape May* he thought, it sounds like my cousin Marilyn.

Normally the speed of the golf carts would have been an impediment to the other trucks and autos sharing the highway, but the whole group was just inching along. You could tell that there were a lot of drivers from the northeast and Miami from the constant sounding of horns and shouts as if that could make things move faster. Not.

In Cocoa Beach a horn tooter was met with disparagement and "Snowbird", but not road rage.

Mikey and Sherri passed under I-75 and were pretty much in the clear until they were almost to the coast. People were getting desperate for gas, and Mikey wanted to tank up because it might be their last chance for a couple of days.

The line for the large discount station essentially had the right lane backed up for a quarter of a mile, but after about twenty minutes they were next in line at the pump. The young man who occupied the pump ahead of them was oblivious to the urgency felt by others in line. He had slowly exited his pickup and first checked his cell phone before casually deciding on the appropriate credit card. Finally he started pumping with the nozzle latch in place while he continued to check messages from IT land.

There was a buzz in the air. In the next lane a larger pickup was finishing fueling UNTIL the owner pulled six five gallon portable plastic containers from the cargo bed. At this point the driver awaiting his turn lost it. Jumping out of his truck he untangled a large knife which could have been a short machete. Without losing a breath he told the fellow with six storage cans that he was about to lose his male organ, after which the knife wielder intended to fill the offender to the nostrils with high test and place a wick in his mouth, that wick being his aforementioned removed male organ.

There was a good side to this story as far as Mikey was concerned, because the young cell phone operator ahead of Mikey shut off the pump, and left the pump ready for Mikey to get gas before it ran out. The other good results was the police car and ambulance racing to the scene created a clear path for Mikey, Sherri and Lulu to cruise safely out of the gas station and down the road to their motel.

After some difficulty in locating the road to the Scallop Harbor Resort they pulled into the driveway of an older but well-kept multi building motel complex. A sign advertised 'fine dining and fresh seafood' as well as tours and snorkeling trips 'with the mermaids', which were actually manatees.

There was mild panic at the small registration desk when the receptionist had difficulty finding the reservation which Sherri had made on line and then confirmed by telephone. The receptionist was a pleasant soft spoken mid-eastern woman,

"I am sorry, but I do not seem to have a reservation. When did you make it?" she asked.

"Well, I did it on line and then spoke to someone on the phone," Sherri said as a puff of smoke emitted from her ear.

"Ah, here is the owner, he can help,"

The owner had a severe look. Standing about five inches taller than Mikey, but eyeball to eyeball with Sherri, he straightend his newly ironed long sleeve shirt and asked with a heavy guttural accent "Whaaat is de probelem??"

Sensing the manager was uncomfortable, Mikey eased his way into the conversation,

"I hope we can find a place to stay here as we DID make a reservation and there are no other motels available that take pets, pointing to Lulu smiling at the open car window. My wife has just had a surgery and we really can't go much further."

The owner took a deep breath, "I can sympathize with you as a few years ago I had a similar situation. I am from Afghanistan and the war was very harsh on my family. We sought refuge at the American embassy. They asked me what was my occupation and I honestly replied that I was a farmer. The officer soldier and a civilian man asked me what I grew and I said "Opium". In no time they rewarded my honesty with some money and moved us to America."

Mikey replied "I have been to that part of the world many times but of course not to

Afghanistan because I was a seaman and there are no ports in Afghanistan."

The owner was impressed, "so you are familiar with that part of the world. That is unusual for most Americans except for military. Let me ask you a question, 'Are the Taliban Sunni or Shiite?'"

Without hesitation Mikey said "Sunni".

The owner smiled and pensively continued, "Ahh it seems you have passed ze test. I do have a room for you and your wife AND your dog. It is not very fancy, we call it THE MANGER..."

Taken back a bit Mikey asked, "Why do you call it The Manger?"

"Well, because it is for people who sleep with animals and pets, which I believe is a similar story from your Bible," he replied, but I have heard that the storm track is changing and may be coming here instead of the east coast, so be ready to move if the local police come. I must go now as the bank will be closing...and by the way we have excellent scallops. The season just started."

"Thank you, I would like to have some tea with you sir, and may I ask your name?" Mikey replied.

"Muhammed Abdul Hussein, and yours...ahh yes right here on the card, Mikey Burkus. Unusual name. What is it? "

"American of Irish, Polish and Roman descent."

"Very good, until later."

THE MANGER

The room, aka "The Manger" was basic but clean with a TV and microwave,

"Not bad," said Mikey. "I'll bet some Syrian refugees would love this place."

After getting half way settled Sherri took Lulu for a walk. There were three men at the dock hurriedly getting several boats firmly tied up and cleaning up loose buckets and fishing equipment.

One of the men greeted Sherri, "This storm is going to be a bad start to the scalloping."

"Do you have any scallop shells?" asked Sherri.

"Only about a thousand," he replied, "would you like a couple?"

Jackpot!

The fisherman whose name was Joe, graciously stopped what he was doing and led her to the cleaning table about forty feet away. Joe gave her about two hundred perfect shells in an old string bag.

"What are you going to do with these?" he asked.

"Well, we live in Cocoa Beach and I paint the shells and sell them at the farmer's market on Saturday along with some painted coconuts. The rest of the painted shells I give to my husband who gives them to people that he meets on the beach as thanks for helping to keep the beach clean. We evacuated across state because of the storm track."

Joe stopped bagging the shells and turned to look Sherri in the eye. "Then you haven't heard?? IRMA is now predicted to go right through here in about two and a half days. The police will be around soon because this place gets under water in a hurry!!"

Sherri thanked Joe warmly and hurried Lulu back to the manger. Mikey had already seen the news on the weather channel and was waiting for the girls.

"Hey, if Jim Cantore says he is coming to your location you know it's time to leave. I don't know what we should do. The highways are jammed and there probably isn't a room to be had this side of Tennessee that will take a dog. I had better get us a meal and talk to Muhammed."

Muhammed was not at the desk. Several people were standing around the small lobby, some looking for a room and some wanting to check out and risk their luck on the road. It was late afternoon, so Mikey decided to try the small restaurant in case they decided to close. The well-traveled waitress forced a smile as Mikey ordered a large scallop dinner take out. Her name tag said Marlene.

"Well, I was counting on a big crowd for the scallop season, but the cops have been around already telling us the evacuation is going mandatory pretty soon ," Marlene said.

Then Mikey saw a vaguely familiar well-dressed woman and two other ladies that had finished their dinner and were departing. He cautiously approached the group.

"Aren't you Sarah?" Mikey asked.

The woman smiled.

"I might be," she said, "and who might YOU

be?".

"Well, about five years ago I was a dancer with a group called the Tripndales. We were dancing at a ladies club in Miami, I think it was called the Old Bag Mitzvahs, when you ..."

"You're the guy I pulled off the runway and pulled down your camouflaged speedo !!! How could I forget? My Gawd. Some Padorkus!!."

"Oh yeah, and then you announced to the world that He ain't Jewish and you hustled me out the door into the hotel hallway."

"Then I yelled No Tips," " Sarah announced to her girlfriends.

"What was your dancer name again?"

"GIGANTICUS PADORKUS" Mikey replied.

"Well," Sarah relented, "I was pretty loaded that night...and what are you doing now Mister Padorkus?" she asked with a cautious flirtatious smile.

"Picking up some stuff for my wife, we just drove over from Cocoa Beach and it appears that we are getting a mandatory boot tonight."

Sarah sighed a disappointed sigh.

"Oh, well nice to see you. Good to see you again, in a manner of speaking," said Sarah as she headed for the parking lot with her girlfriends, glancing back as she walked out the door telling the story once again to her giggling girlfriends.

It didn't take long for the mandatory order to leave arrived. Back in The Manger they were just finishing the scallops when a bull horn in the parking lot blared "mandatory evacuation, all guests must leave", followed by a knock on the door. Sherri answered the knock to be greeted by two officers, one in SWAT gear and the other, a well decorated uniformed police officer. It was the Sheriff.

"Sorry m'am, but y'all must leave," the Sheriff said. His badge identified him as Sheriff Harold Greatly, who was known in the county as 'Harold the Great'.

"Y'all just missed dinner," Sherri said.

Mikey said nothing as they had agreed a long time ago that New Jersey accents didn't always work south of Maryland. Florida is south of Georgia.

"We were just getting ready when y'all came since we had just arrived from mandatory evacuation from Cocoa Beach", Sherri smiled politely.

"Y'all have any ideas which way to go Sheriff Greatly? My late father was a retired Virginia State Trooper and my husband is a retired veteran."

"Well, the highways are jammed, there aren't any hotels from here to Tennessee that I know of, and the storm is coming here," which was not much help from Harold the Great.

"I think we might just as well head back home," Mikey chimed in, which was greeted with "Are youse from New Joisey?" from the Sheriff.

"Yes, but I am converted, big admirer of Stonewall Jackson AND Bobby Lee," Then Mikey slipped Harold the Great the secret handshake he had learned from his late father-in-law and everything was friendly.

"Ok, folks. I can give you an hour to leave, but that's about it. Have a safe trip." and then they were gone with bullhorns and sirens filling the evening calm, followed by a multimillion dollar SWAT car and a fire engine with the Sheriff's helo flying close support overhead."

Sherri called the Cocoa Beach police info line and was thankfully told that the causeways to Cocoa Beach were still open and would probably remain so for at least 24 hours. They quickly finished packing and the little band of refugees headed back across state. The north/south highways were jammed, but cross state was wide open and just before midnight they arrived back home in Cocoa Beach. Surprisingly the parking area next to their townhouse was half full. The majority of the neighbors had stayed or eventually decided to give up on the traffic and return home to ride out IRMA. Now the neighbors greeted the small group of innocents clear of the control of Harold the Great.

Final preparations were made the next day

and before long the skies darkened, the wind picked up and lightning flashed above. The lightning was followed by the low rumble of thunder like Civil War artillery announcing the opening salvo of battle. Boom, boom, boom boom!!

IRMA lived up to her reputation as a very large and powerful hurricane, and although sixty some miles east of the eye, powerful winds and rain shook the community. The local news tracked about 25 mini tornadoes passing north and south of their townhouse, and then one came down about 100 yards to the east, skipped over Mikey's place touched down again, decimating two ancient oak trees blocking the roads to the community. Their eight foot high wooden patio privacy fence began to wave like a slinky and partially disintegrated into flying debris, a piece of which got forced through the air conditioner fan which then seized with a very loud bang. Before long the lights went out and would not come on again for days. Comparatively speaking to other places in Florida and Houston, and later Puerto Rico, they had it easy. No deaths, no injuries and no real flooding even though the beach was two hundred yards away. The sand dunes which were maintained mostly by local volunteers had done their job.

The morning light was cautiously greeted as the neighbors opened their storm shutters and stepped outside to assess the damage.

"Not too bad, not too bad, what are you guys doing back, who has electricity? Nobody. Who has water?   Nobody, except for the water in the bath tub and about five cases of bottles and gallon jugs."

"Who has coffee?" We do, heating up some water on the grill, ok, anybody hurt? Nope. The positive sounds of relief and faces with frayed hair, backward turned baseball hats and reflected exhaustion slowly came together at JB and Jill's patio where water boiled on the gas grill and instant coffee toasted the morning. JB fried up a huge pan of eggs. For the next five days the community persevered using buckets of water from the swimming pool for toilet flushing, and the pool itself for cooling off in the ninety degree heat. Personal autos and power packs also provided power for cell phone charging and, when desperately needed, short term air conditioning. Power packs were the best source for powering up electronic stuff. Sherri and Lulu slept on air mattresses outside on the second floor balcony while Mikey slept inside. Mikey kept his six shooter nearby in the event of looters, "If there be looters I got a six shooter," he growled. Mikey and Sherri listened to music on the battery radio. In a couple of days there were newspapers at stores powered by emergency generators. When the power came back on the little community jumped into the pool. Mrs. Rosenburg had the most wrinkles. Mikey suggested group sex which caused Mrs. O'Reilly to barf, luckily not in the pool.

The weeks that followed were busy and bitter- sweet. More than half of the Beach had been eroded, leaving trash of kinds and numbers Mikey had not previously seen. After three days a deceased four foot logger head turtle lay on its back as the tide went out. Mikey helped Maggie bag up the beautiful creature. It gave Mikey a sense of closure that picking up the trash helped save other creatures from a similar fate. The loggerhead's stomach was later found to be filled with plastic and other non-digestible debris.

Mikey and Sherri's annual pilgrimage to the Florida Keys was on hold. Usually September and October were good dates as the rents were still at seasonable low. It was also lobster and stone crab season. In addition to the variety of fresh fish and beautiful water it was a great break at a reasonable price. Unfortunately a week after IRMA's wrath had left, and hurricane MARIA was tearing her way through the Caribbean, they received a disappointing phone call from Javier, a Cuban American friend and the owner of their rental.

"Mikey, I'll be sending your money back this week when I get back to Miami," said Javier.

"We thought the building was sound but today the roof collapsed and it is a total loss."

"I am very sad for you Javier and I hope that you and your family are safe. What about Dorothy and Charles?" Mikey asked.

"Their place was one of the few that survived,

but they are sleeping in their little camper away from the water as the decaying seaweed stench is very bad. They said it is like sleeping in a manger."

"We can relate to that," Mikey interjected.

Javier continued, "The storm surge was so powerful that at least six homes were swept from their foundations and we have no idea where they are except part of the billion splinters and trash that have contaminated the area. The wave actually picked up the huge boulders from the jetty and washed them through the houses.   Remember Manny? They found what was left of his boat still in the cradle with the davit about half a mile away," Javier replied sadly.

"Well, Javier, we shall get down somehow and in the meantime please say hello to our friends. Be safe amigo."

"Thank you my friend," Javier replied.

PARADISE LOST

Every year Sherri looked forward to the Keys trip. It was about 250 miles from Cocoa Beach to Key Largo including about fifty hair raising miles of Florida turnpike driving through Miami. The highway with no rules.

Although the beaches were far from being as beautiful as Cocoa Beach, the beautiful water, great seafood and developed friendships were a precious part of her life. She became very depressed and remained so for a couple of days, but within a week their rent and deposit had returned in full via mail. Javier was a man of his word. His family had fled Cuba around 1960 and he was a successful business man. Mikey had always had a good relationship with the Cuban Americans from his days as captain of a small cargo ship which ran to Central and South America from Fort Lauderdale and Lake Charles, Louisiana. He had picked up around forty total Ballesteros, boat people, in those ten years and remained in touch with several of the families.

Now IRMA and MARIA were going to

change the demographics of Florida and to a lesser extent the United States. They started to look for an alternate rental somewhere, anywhere in the Keys. Their vacation could be a working vacation to help out IRMA's survivors.

Mikey went back to cleaning up beach trash. There was plenty of it, big stuff like insulation and trees that were uprooted elsewhere and floated north in the Gulf Stream and stranded ashore on high tide.

About a month later they were still looking for a spot in the Keys. The Puerto Rican situation was desperate. Sherri asked Mikey, "Who will step up and rebuild Puerto Rico? Who has the money?"

Mikey put down his coffee and looked at Sherri with a solemn face, "The Chinese. It isn't the media's tragedy of the week yet, but the Chinese are building their own Trans-Nicaragua Canal, and have built a Trans-Costa Rican highway. They are developing ports on the east and west coast of Costa Rica and Nicaragua which will also give them spheres of influence, which in turn will provide support of their growing Navy. To buy Puerto Rico all they have to do is cash in some of their US treasury securities, pay off the right people and there you go. "

"Mikey, how you know all this?" asked Sherri. "Who would try to sell Puerto Rico to the Chinese? It is part of America for God's sake."

"Well, it appears to me that there are many powerful politicians who don't even consider Puerto Ricans as Americans because of their Hispanic heritage and Caribbean life style. Maybe if they were Norwegians they would get a better fantastic deal."

There was plenty of work to be done in Cocoa Beach, but Mikey and Sherri decided to find a place somewhere in the Keys. Sherri's internet skills located the owner of one of their previous rentals in Key Largo, but it too was unlivable because of roof damage. The owner was able to set them up on another bayside canal location with a vintage pontoon boat to go along with the rental. They would be going down in a couple of days. No sooner than the moment they began to pack, their next door neighbor Billie called.   She said that Beatrice needed some help getting to the market. Beatrice lived by herself in an adjacent town house. Billie had her own hair styling salon and was just getting it ready to reopen. Her husband James was busy remodeling and fixing houses. Three other neighbors spent tons of time and devotion keeping the old gal going, but today it fell to Mikey. He walked to her unit and knocked on the gate which had a large wooden yellow bumble bee hanging on the gate.

"Hey Bea, wassup!"

Bea was hard core Bostonian, somewhere around eighty-five years old. She had been widowed for over thirty-five years, and scraped by on social security and some meager savings. Her pleasure in life was taking a weekly day trip on the local gambling boat to splurge twenty-five dollars on the penny slots. She usually had multiple dark bruises from a combination of falling, blood thinner and a broad spectrum of other medicines and currently was sporting her left arm in a sling. Her gnarled arthritic hands and twisted fingers reminded Mikey of Mother

Theresa and ET. She called Mikey "Captain Midnight"!

"Captain Midnight we have to get to the super market this afternoon because it is the last day of the hurricane specials, and I have coupons for all that I need."

"Okay, I'll get my car, "said Mikey.

"No, no we have to go in my car, because that is where I have my wheel chair if we need it, and it is easy for me to get out of the car," Bea replied.

"Well, why don't I just go for you," Mikey ventured.

"No, no you might get the wrong stuff and it is the last day."

So they got Bea's walker and shuffled down to the early eighties vintage station wagon with less than 70,000 original miles on the odometer. It was beige brown with a few rust spots from the salt and sun exposure. Mikey held the door and Bee lowered herself into the passenger seat and said, "Thank you Captain Midnight."

She had driven herself until recently when her macular eye degeneration became advanced making driving very unsafe for Bea and the community at large. Her son Jimmy and his family had frequently asked Bea to come and live with them in Maine, but she preferred the warm weather, her church friends and the gambling boat as well as occasional sorties to the card rooms in nearby Melbourne.

"My family has plenty of things on their own plate," Bea said. "Kids in school, his wife has been ill, and Jimmy just got his Doctorate and a promotion. I would be a burden and spend my time looking out the window at the woods in the summer and the snow in the winter."

They drove the five blocks to the supermarket and were lucky to find a handicapped spot near the door. Mikey suggested a motorized shopping cart but that was vetoed, and Bea took her position firmly behind the push shopping cart while Mikey acted as a tug boat slowly pulling them along. "Vegetable department first," announced Bea. "How much are the tomatoes?"

"One twenty-nine a pound?"

"Too much? Check the coupon"

"OK. One ten a pound."

"I'll get one"

"Where's the bananas?' asked Bea.

"Right here, special for thirty-nine cents a bag, but they're pretty black"

"Get five bags,"

Mikey stopped. "What are you going to do with all of those bananas?"

"Freeze them!" Bea replied.

Mikey shook his head.

"Okay, now the wine department."

After a short shuffling transit they arrived at the gallon jugs of red wine on sale for eight ninety-five a gallon. "The good stuff thought Mikey.

"Get six gallons."

"Chianti or Ruffino?" Mikey asked.

"Doesn't matter as long as we get six gallons".

The shopping adventure was completed with twenty-one containers of yogurt, various flavors, which were about to expire and were selling for three containers for the price of one. Last was a gallon of bargain chocolate ice cream, "Gotta have my dairy," said Bea.

"Do you have a sugar diabetes problem, Miss Bea?"

"I don't think so. But I have everything else."

Shortly they shuffled up to the check-out manned by a pleasant middle aged woman. The bagger was a younger haggard looking girl. Both looked at the shopping basket contents, Bea's bruises and the sling on her arm from which she was sliding out coupons with her good wrinkled hand.

It was one of those moments that Mikey couldn't resist.

"You may wonder about our food selection today," he said.

The checkout woman silently acknowledged his question.

"Bea runs a rehabilitation center for alcoholic

monkeys and chimps in her condo. She puts them slowly in withdrawal by lacing the bananas with small amounts of red wine. Later they progress to yogurt and finally to ice cream before we return them to their owners or to the Zoo."

Bea acted like she hadn't heard a word as she was focused on her coupons.

"Well, that is very nice," said the checkout lady.

"What about the bruises and broken arm," asked the suspicious bagger girl?

Mikey let out a sigh. "It's those darn mean monkeys always hitting her," Mikey replied. The bagger girl looked forlornly at Bea as she helped them to the parking spot. With Bea reinstalled in the front seat Mikey and the bagger girl loaded up the back of the station wagon and gently closed the hatch back as to not damage the gallons of wine. Then the tired bagger girl looked Mikey in the eye and said, "I hope the monkeys behave themselves and they all get better y'all. I hope they all make it."

"Y'all take care," said Mikey.

As they headed back to the townhouse complex Bea softly smiled as she looked down the road, "You know I heard everything that you said about my rehab center, where do you come up with your bullshit stories, Captain Midnight???"

"It's a gift", said Mikey, "How about I help you with the groceries and talk about it."

I COULDA BEEN A GANGSTA

The groceries were put away and Bea worked herself to her easy chair recliner. She had poured herself a small glass of wine and showed Mikey her coffee pot stash. In a few minutes he settled down on the couch with a fresh cup of mud.

Mikey started," Bea, I have been asked many times why or where I get my stories. I have in fact kissed the Blarney stone at Blarney Castle. Have you ever been there?"

"No, I never made it."

"Well, never say that the Irish are dumb. The castle and the grounds are beautiful and one pays about twelve euros admission. If one decides to kiss the Blarney stone you climb a narrow winding ancient tower stairway made of much worn stones to the top of what I guess might be called a parapet. Arriving at the top exit of the tower you then walk about half way around the parapet to *THE STONE*, BAARAAA. "

"Are you all alone?" asked Bea, "because I

don't know if I could do all of those stairs?"

"No, when I was there the line was a continuous parade, but many chose to not climb the stairs"

"Then I wouldn't feel strange or out of place?"

"Oh, not at all, " comforted Mikey.

"Then maybe I'll get there some day," she speculated.

"Could be" Mikey agreed, "but there is more to it."

"So you get around the parapet to *THE STONE* and there is a local fellow sitting on the edge of an opening in the walkway. They tell you that you can take a pictures, but pretty soon you figure out this is very impractical. When you reach the head of the line you turnaround and lay down. You drop a Euro or two in the local fellow's hat and he holds your waist or legs and you slide out under the parapet opening and raise yourself up to kiss the stone. As you do you are aware of your photograph being taken."

Bea smiled impishly. "It sounds like an

acrobatic act of some sort."

"I thought so myself". Mikey paused. "The final surprise is after you descend another weathered stone stairwell, you then exit into the arms of the photographer who has your pictures developed and there you are in full glory kissing the Blarney Stone."

"Fifteen more euros for two," he politely says with a smile and a handshake.

"Of course I have a framed picture of THE act, and I often think of how much money those sly Irish are making on people willing to kiss a stone in a contortioned manner."

Bea paused, "but that isn't where you get all of your story telling talent?"

"No" Mikey replied," I must say it is a reflection of my father and to a lesser extent my mother. My father Harry Burke was a young newspaper reporter in the '30s in Newark, New Jersey. During his life he worked for a total of about 45 years for the *Newark Evening News*. His father, I was told, was one of the first reporters and editors of the *Newark Star Ledger*. I never met my grandfather. In any case part of my father's 'beat' as they call it, was Newark City Hospital. One day the gangster Dutch Schultz was shot and badly wounded, and then taken to Newark City Hospital. My father tried to gain access but was locked out until he spotted two nurses, one of which he had met at a speakeasy. They got him in the back door and my father was able to get Schultz's last words. That story elevated him from 'cub' reporter to a more sophisticated 'beat'. Because Schultz was Jewish, my father somehow became the confident of many of the Jewish and later Italian mobsters in the city. They trusted him because he never violated a confidence. When you said "This is off the record" to Harry Burke, it was not leaked. In this way he became a sometimes unplanned messenger between the underworld, labor leaders and local politicians. At his funeral one very trusted and honest Teamster Official took me aside and told me that he was known as 'the String' with certain people. It was special for me because one of the nurses became my Mother."

"Most of my father's friends were journalists, photographers and the many colorful and sometimes notorious characters around northern New Jersey. They were mostly survivors of the Great Depression and/or veterans of WWII combat. I would listen to their stories and adventures whenever they got together at social and family gatherings, or when my father would have me take a bus to the newspaper building and meet him for lunch and to show me off. He did the same for my late brother Harry Jr. who was seven years younger than I.

I met and shook hands with many of the sometimes questionable celebrities, and impatiently waited for the newspaper to arrive at the stoop in the afternoon where my mother and I would comb the pages in search of his "by line", that is "By Harry Burke".

"What kind of people were these?" Bea asked.

"Well, the author of Uncle Wiggly, Howard Garris was one. Boxers in a gym, former bootleggers in a bar, powerful labor leaders, G-men, and politicians. There was one guy named "Nylon Jake" who could get you anything. He wore a big trench coat and when he opened it up there were nylon stockings, small hams and cigarettes. The fact that I could read at an early age really was a factor."

"Well then Captain Midnight, why didn't you become a reporter like your father?"

Mikey thought before answering.

"As I grew up many of the people I mentioned took a shine to me, and there was always a favor, a job, an introduction, maybe even tuition, that I was able to get because I was 'Harry's Kid Michael.' This got me part time jobs as an ironworker, teamster loading ice cream trucks, operating engineer and department store stock clerk. It also got me out of a couple of scrapes with the law. But in the fall of 1962 I was a recent college grad on my way to law school when the Cuban situation began to boil over. The draft board said my number was coming up, and for a lot of reasons I wanted to be a sailor, not a soldier. So I enlisted in the Navy without telling my parents because JFK said, '...ask NOT what your country can do for you ask what you can do for your country...' and because I wanted to be my own person and not 'Harry's Kid Michael'.

"As simple as that?" asked Bea.

Mikey pondered the question. "Not really. The other gigantic influence on my moral fiber was the four years that I spent at Saint Benedict's prep, an inner city boy's school run by Benedictine monks, right in the middle of Newark. There I was molded into a young man by exceptional priests, and made some of the best friends a person could ever hope to know. We still stay in touch after sixty years."

"Other than that it was as simple as that. Maybe there was a broken heart involved somewhere in there. So shortly after I enlisted the recruiter calls up and asks would I consider being an officer?"

"At first I was reluctant because it meant three years in the Navy instead of two. A lot of my friends were avoiding the draft with deferments, bone spurs and political connections. They thought I was a chump for enlisting in the first place. So I spoke to a very special priest from Saint Benedict's.

"Michael, I think you should be an officer and be the best officer that you can be.   I later discovered that he was, I believe, an officer in WWII.   Life's unseen circle."

"I guess you liked it," said Bea.

"Oh yes I did, and I stayed for twenty years as a line officer, got a command, was Chief Engineer three times, and had a lot of great experiences, not to mention a pension, and a drinking problem."

"There were the tough times too," Mikey continued, "as there are in all lives and occupations. After twenty I retired but could not settle into civilian life, so I was able to sit for an Unlimited Merchant Marine Captain's ticket and I did, and then I spent thirty more years as a deck officer and ship's Captain as well as a maritime school instructor in my later years."

"You got divorced twice?' interjected Bea.

"Very sad, I was in the 'catch and release program'. But my drinking and never ending desire for another 'adventure' as I called it, were the big reasons. And Vietnam with four deployments over five years. I don't like to talk about it."

"I wasn't a good father. My son Matt called me the Great Santini."

"So does that explain why you are so off the wall sometimes?" asked Bea.

"That's what I think. I have been so many places and seen and done so many things, ate so much great food and met so many people of all flavors all over the world that I just try to put a bit of levity into life when people seem so unhappy. The joyful participation in the sorrows of life."

"Was there one particular event that you can recall?" asked Bea.

Standing up and looking out the patio door, Mikey pulled up a story from the back of his tattered brain.

"Oh, there were several. My last assignment in the Navy was command of an ammunition ship. I had my own Filipino steward who cooked my food and took care of all my personal needs. A long way from Newark.

I always got along with the Filipinos and called them by their name not 'Steward' as I heard some junior officers do on my first ship. Anyway, Sampson was my personal steward. A kind and gentle family man. One day the Supply officer assigned a brand new Filipino steward's assistant, fresh from the Philippines via boot camp, to work with Sampson for a while and get acquainted with shipboard life. This kid could eat. In fact his name was Comer, 'to eat'.

One day after a couple of weeks of familiarization both Sampson and Comer were doing something around my office and I took the opportunity to see how things were going. Comer said in broken English, 'Good, I like the America'. (We were tied up in San Francisco).

Then hesitantly said, 'everybody has toilet, house, car, TV, food, everything. I just no understand why a lot of people always complaining.'

"So it was sitting at the feet of these great literary minds that planted the seed and fruition".

"Profound" observed Bea.

Mikey took a small step towards the door. "I'll see you when we get back from the Keys, Bea."

"Can you bring me a small lobsta?"

"I'll bring you two," giving her a hug as he walked out the door.

KEY LARGO

It was a beautiful morning as Mikey and Sherri finished packing the SUV with extra food and survival things and left Cocoa Beach for Key Largo. They had lingered an extra day hoping to see Sherri's special friend Joanna from Iceland but somehow the connections got crossed up and they missed her. "Loading this tricycle on the back of the SUV is the toughest part of the trip," Mikey said.

"I agree, do you think we need some help?" answered Sherri.

Just then their neighbors Lucy and her husband Adam came by. Adam is a big Rugby player and Lucy is an engineer. The pair analyzed the complexities of the bike rack and had everything loaded and secured in five minutes followed by some tweaking. Lulu was running around in anticipation of the trip and was loaded into a comfortable back seat bed. Then it was check all the lights and doors and hot water heater and the little band of adventurers were on the road again.

'I'll drive as long as I can," said Mikey.

Sherri had an anxiety problem with the highway traffic. In the past they had a travel trailer pulled by a V-8 Tundra. One summer they had done an 11,000 mile circumnavigation of the country. Now it was a bit too strenuous and the truck and travel trailer were gone.

"I keep looking out the back window to see if the trailer is back there," reminisced Sherri.

"Yeah," said Mikey, "we sure have done some traveling."

"Well, you remember that you are not as strong as you were ten years ago," Sherri came back.

"Yes, Master," said Mikey and started making belly dancer noises, "No more beatings."

The first two hours were easy, but then I-95 turned into the south Florida megalopolis and the next hour was no rules or speed limit, road rage permitted especially through the Miami construction zones. Sherri decided to lay down in the back seat with Lulu and try to relax, but every time the shadow of a maniac speeder or eighteen wheeler passed by her anxiety increased. Finally, they reached the end of the Florida turnpike in Florida City, with nothing remaining but US Route One south and the Florida Keys.

The tranquility lasted about three minutes as traffic came to a halt and flashing lights were everywhere.

"I hope they haven't shut down the road," said Sherri. "I can't take much more of this."

"We are being detoured, but still heading south," said Mikey trying not to get distracted as traffic was redirected through a strip mall and service station parking lot, and then exited back on the highway where they saw the problem. A gigantic cement electrical transmission pole mounted on special oversize trucks had jack knifed trying to make a U-turn. There were several officials and law enforcement officers scratching their heads. They seemed to be listening to a man in a leather jacket and jeans. It was a familiar face.

"Hey, it's John Boy," shouted Sherri as she rolled down the back window and shouted out her greeting. "Straighten this mess out John Boy!!" as they slowly passed by in the detoured procession.

The officers looked in their direction and Sherri was about to flip them off. Mikey yelled "NO!" just in time. "See you in Key Largo John, we'll text you later."

"Ok", John Boy shouted back and returned to the road block.

Now the road ahead was clear and moving down the twenty miles to Key Largo.

In this area essentially both sides of route one are fenced off. There is sparse building to protect the land from the people and the people from the land, the gators and more recently the snakes. It is a one lane divided highway in both directions separated by cement barriers with an occasional passing zone or turn off. If you get behind a slow moving camper or boat being towed, then you have to jockey around them in the passing lanes. Thankfully the beautiful aquamarine water soon came into view and they crossed the Jewfish River Bridge and arrived in Key Largo at mile marker 106.

The mile marker at the furthest point south in Key West is zero. You find your location along US 1 by knowing the Mile Marker.

"Man, look at that traffic going north," observed Sherri.

"Trash trucks, campers, boats, flat beds with damaged cars. So sad." She teared up. "We were lucky. These people are leaving and many will never be able to come back to a lifestyle that they loved even if they want to."

Mikey turned right at mm 106 and wove through three streets on the bayside to find the rental.   There was litter and trash along the roads and in backyards.

The owner was waiting outside with his family.

"Hey Stu good to see you," said Mikey.

"You as well." Pointing to his truck he introduced, "This is my wife and daughter. We have to hurry because we had to relocate to Miami until the school situation resolves itself. There are over three hundred homeless kids in my daughter's school alone. No electricity or water at the local schools yet.

Really tough, and these kids are helping out cleaning and fixing when not in school. Jennifer is going to school in Miami for a while."

Jennifer made a fuss over Lulu as they checked out the locks and rules of the rental. The pontoon boat was docked in the narrow canal behind the house. Stu went over the controls with Mikey.

"It might be a little tight getting out of here, Capitano. Your next door neighbor Vito will help you. I think he is from New Jersey".

They returned to the house and found it clean and comfortable.

"Ok Stu, we'll text you if there are any questions. Where do I put this yard trash?"

Stu was a little surprised. "Well, you don't have to clean up, but if you do just pick a pile in the street and it will be collected up twice a week. Try to keep the vegetation and wooden debris separate."

Then Stu and his family were gone to join the crush of northbound traffic.

"This is a great porch and the screens should keep out the bugs and critters," speculated Sherri. "I can paint my shells and coconuts right here."

"Time to kick back and let John Boy know where we are," said Mikey as he checked out the coffee pot.

They slept well after the tough trip. The next morning brought surprises. Mikey being the early riser had Lulu on the leash for a walk. He got off the back porch but almost immediately saw a visitor on the dock and retreated back inside.

"Oh Sherri, We got a veezetor!!"

Still in a daze Sherri growled, "John Boy?"

"I don't know if it is Clarence the crocodile or Gertie the gator, but IT is sunning on the dock. Probably looking for Lulu stew or leg of Sherri for breakfast."

"Where's the dog, where's the dog?" Sherri yelled.

"No worries, right here on her leash. Just thought you should know."

Then Mikey took Lulu out the front door which put them on the street and separated from the canal by a fence.

After about ten minutes of Lulu wearing her nose out with all the new smells they returned home.

"There are a lot of moldy smells in the air. We should take a trip around town to see what is open or, you can stay here and play with the crocodile," said Mikey.

They cruised down the road towards Islamorada. Flattened famous restaurants were now only memories in old photo albums and cell phone cameras. Everywhere there were fifty foot high piles of vegetation, appliances and general building trash inter-dispersed with boats, autos and campers that extended for hundreds of yards. Every park, playground, and parking lot had been commandeered as the residents struggled to clear the roads and home sites.

"Look at that," said Sherri as they arrived in Tavenier and turned left off the highway looking for the Harry Harris Beach on the oceanside. "Looks like a very expensive RV motorhome has parked itself in a tree alongside two boats."

Then to their complete surprise they saw that people were in the RV and one of the boats. Makeshift ladders gave access about ten feet above the ground. A woman was hanging a couple of pieces of clothing from an improvised clothes line. Nearby a man dressed in a bathing suit and flip flops was cooking on a grill underneath but away from the boat. A "Conch Republic" flag waved softly in the breeze. He waved and they stopped.

"What are you touristas doing down here?" he smiled.

Sherri replied because it was y'all time, "Hey, we're from Cocoa Beach and came down to see what was going on and help out if we can y'all."

"Greetings. My name's Sergio. Y'all wouldn't happen to have any water? It's hard to carry water down here on my bike."

There was an almost filled gallon jug in the back and a couple of cool bottles in their travel cooler.

"Here ya go," said Mikey.

"What do I owe you?" asked Sergio.

"Just stay safe and be a friend."

"That's what the Godfather said", answered Sergio. "I knew that you were from Joisey."

Mikey made his best Godfather face and did an imitation that Sergio liked and Sherri gave the "not that again" look.

They waved good bye and headed back toward the beach which was close by.

"I thought that the Conch Republic was Key West," said Sherri.

"Originally it was only Key West when they claimed independence around 1982 I think, but it since has been expanded northward to include most or all of the Keys. They claim to bring more humor, warmth, and respect to a world in sore need of all of these",

"I guess that it why we like it down here," Sherri said as they came to the park gate.

At the end of the road a handwritten sign said 'PARK CLOSED'. There was a lot of trash, but hard to tell if it was deposited by the residents or IRMA.   They sadly made a turn back to route one, stopping at the supermarket strip mall.

Sherri went into the supermarket while Mikey walked Lulu around the large parking lot that had been mostly cleared. Suddenly Lulu went into her hunting alert mode, ears and tail pointed upward.

"CHICKENS!!" exclaimed Mikey.

Apparently many people kept chickens and the storm had relocated about twenty survivors. No roosters, just hens scratching around for food.

Lulu was loaded into the car and Mikey started the engine and air conditioning. Sherri returned shortly with the groceries.

"Did you see the chickens?" she asked.

"Lulu the mighty chicken hunter was ready to take them on."

Lulu gave a dog grin and panted for Sherri to see.

"Mikey did you see that clinic next to the Publix?"

"Just the big sign that said 'Emergency Walk In'."

"It looks pretty nice," said Sherri. "They have a sign listing what drugs they DON'T prescribe. There is another that says 'no credit cards' and an arrow indicating the ATM is next door at the Publix."

'I hope that we don't need them, but it is good to know", reflected Mikey as they maneuvered out of the parking lot and home.

Back at the rental they unpacked the car and checked around for critters. Luckily Clarence the crocodile had moved on.

"We still can do a lot," said Sherri. "There is the Bogart Festival next week and the Stone Crab eating contest in Marathon is at the Fisheries, and I think I am going to repaint all of the metallic lizards and fish on the buildings around here with bright colors to spruce things up."

"Yes and the waters seem clear enough on the bayside that we take the pontoon boat for a little cruise and go snorkeling when we find some nice water," contributed Mikey.

The rest of first week was uneventful as a routine morphed into place. John Boy texted that he was at mm 10 helping out his brother Everett and friends repair and rebuild.

Their next door neighbor turned out to be one of Mikey's contemporaries from northern New Jersey. Remarkably Vito's career was as an operating engineer and Mikey had worked as an apprentice in the same union when not in school. They had a lot in common and many things to talk about from the good old days, both the good and the bad.

It brought back many memories to 'Harry's Boy Michael.'

Sherri painted a coconut for Vito showing him sitting in a huge crane catching a huge fish on the end of the cargo hook.

Then Mikey started to develop an ingrown cyst on the back of his neck which quickly developed into half the size of a golf ball. This meant a trip to the walk-in clinic. It was a one man operation with two nurses. No frills. The doctor said he could lance the growth, but it probably would come back and who knew what was in the air since IRMA.

So it was very skillfully cut out and stitched up and an ugly looking thing sent off to check for cancer. Medicare was accepted. The four visit procedure which cost Mikey an astounding $54, was considerably less than the same procedure elsewhere.

Sherri commented, "That is the way that medical care is supposed to be. Just another reason to love the Conch Republic. The doctor could have soaked a traveling visitor much, much more."

"Agreed," said Mikey.

They got a couple of trips on the boat, Lulu came along as usual. She seemed to love it all.

Next order of business was to travel to Conch Key and check out their old rental. Things along the highway got even worse after Tavenier. Finally, they turned left at mm 62. The entrance to Conch Key was now guarded by two over turned forty foot trailer trucks. Immediately they saw the remains of their former residence, three piles of gravel and a bulldozer to push the gravel into the gaping hole which had been the beach. The house was gone. Their old neighbors Dorothy and Charles greeted them with handshakes and hugs. Their mobile home had survived while all of the others had just disappeared or were part of the splintered debris. Hand written For Sale signs resembled grave markers on leveled lots. This would require a lot more than Mikey's blue bucket.

Happily Dorothy and Charles' pet box turtle had squeezed her one foot long body into her little house and survived. That still didn't stop Lulu from going into attack mode.

After an hour of hearing the harrowing storm damage stories, Mikey and Sherri were ready to go.

It was all too much and there was really no place to stay as displaced residences and recovery workers were sleeping in their cars and tents.

They said their good byes and headed back to Key Largo counting their blessings.

Then things went downhill rapidly. On the way north Lulu started to cough. By the time they were back in Key Largo Lulu was gagging. She had gone from chasing chickens and threatening crocodiles to barely able to stand.

On their arrival in Key Largo there was a phone call from Billie that Bea had passed away.

It was a no brainer to make the decision to cut their vacation short.

Sherri held Lulu in the back seat for a while and then switched to driving once past Miami. They were first in line when their vet at Aloha Dog Hospital opened at 7 am the next day. The diagnosis was pneumonia or a new strain of mold infection acquired in the Keys. Her condition was bad, but not yet life threatening. After getting a huge dose of antibiotics Lulu was loaded into the car and they headed the fourteen miles to home.

For a couple of days Lulu was fed through a syringe with baby's mother's milk. Mikey made fresh chicken soup and she liked that, syringe or not. She seemed a bit stronger so when morning came they took her out in the patio.

Lulu was laying on the tile deck when Billie's black male cat Pyro went sliding by outside the fence, just to tease the dog. Almost simultaneously a squirrel bounced down the top of the fence.

BOING!!

Lulu sprang to her feet and started running around the fence while trying to attack the two potential invaders. Mikey and Sherri were laughing and crying at the same time.

Mikey tearfully exclaimed, "...and the Oscar for the best acting by a dog goes to ""Lulu""!!!

WHAT EVER HAPPENED TO CHRISTMAS?

In spite of the destruction brought upon the community in general, the Cocoa Beachies, like their Conch Republic brothers, were digging in to make it a Merry and Holy Christmas. Mikey and Sherri put up their little artificial tree which they had for at least ten years, and placed a simple manger fashioned from driftwood on the dining room sideboard. It was their custom to welcome people to their home who really had no family, or place to go, or the money to celebrate with a Christmas Dinner. Bea had been a regular, but she was gone. In the past they had a German cook, Joseph, who worked at a local restaurant and barely knew much English. He brought wine and music. This year a couple Don and Melissa, who had worked with Sherri at the plumbers were at loose ends and also their neighbor Steve who had missed his usual Key West rental to storm damage.

"What ever happened to Christmas?" Steve

asked after sitting at the outside patio table and acknowledging the usual introductions. There were appetizers and plenty to drink, both alcohol and 'no-grape' as Mikey called the non- alcohol beverages.

Don and Melissa were a quiet couple and waited for Mikey to answer. Sherri held her breath.

"Oh, I know what you mean," started Mikey, "The commercialization. But things are going to change, I hear,"

"What did you hear?" asked Sherri cautiously.

"Well, Santa is being bought out by one of the big conglomerates and is moving to this area, probably between here and Orlando."

"Why would Santa do that?" asked Steve.

"It seems that global warming has reached the extent that Santa no longer has a snowy runway guaranteed at Christmas time at the North Pole."

"Well there isn't any snow here," Don chuckled.

"There are other things," continued Mikey. "The Elves are getting older and Santa has lost most of his health care coverage. Polar bears are foraging around the North Pole and one recently attacked Mrs. Claus and a couple of elves while that were out feeding the reindeer. So this conglomerate executive got in touch with Santa, and offered him a non-hostile buyout. Santa would still be in control and direct operations. He also would still be the one who decides who has been naughty or nice."

"Still haven't got any snow in Orlando," said Melissa.

"This is where technology will come in. The aging reindeer will be replaced by drones called Reindrones. They will be able to locate at various locations worldwide and be able to satisfy the requirement to visit every deserving child on Christmas Eve. The drones will operate in squadrons and each squadron will have a leader drone with a red nose who will keep track of deliveries and note any missed deliveries, stuff like that."

Melissa looked worried. "What will happen to

Rudolph and the other Reindeer?"

"No worries," answered Mikey, "they will all be retired to safe pasture with plenty of food and veterinarian care. Rudolph will be making cameo appearances at children's hospitals. Santa doesn't want, or so I am told, to get him shot down by a rogue drone."

Sherri joined the conversation. There were a couple of things that really upset her. Her personality reflected her concern for the working person and the underprivileged. She was especially moved by the plight of the sad and defenseless faces that she saw on the SPCA advertisements on television. Many times she would watch the millionaire politicians giving TV appearances and say, "If I ever had the chance to stand up and talk to a president or governor or whatever I would ask them 'How much does a loaf of bread or a gallon of milk cost and how does a person making less than survival wages pay for food, childcare, rent, healthcare when they hardly make it with both parents working two jobs?

It would break my heart if the joy of

Christmas was left to corporate decisions."

Mikey tried to calm things down. "I don't think that is going to happen, but you never know. Hey look, there's a drone now!!"

The drone flew above the outdoor patio at about a hundred feet. It was decorated with red and green flashing lights and trailing a banner which read "Happy Birthday Baby Jesus!"

The group was silent and there were a few tears.

"Maybe the drones can save Christmas," said Mikey. "It was only a couple of months ago that Sherri and Lulu and I were sleeping in a manger, right Lulu".

Lulu's ears perked up and she barked a few woofs at the drone. Then she ran around the patio making attempts to climb the fence.

Just then James and Billie appeared at the gate. "Just stopping by to wish you a Happy Christmas. We just had our tofu turkey." There was silence as the carnivores contemplated a tofu turkey. "We're on our way to see family and hope you have a good one."

"We shall," replied the carnivores.

As they departed JB and Jill stuck their head in the gate. They were headed out to Kissimmee to visit relatives too. JB asked "Hey, did you ever get that problem with the Space Center straightened out?"

"No worries," said Mikey. "I told them I knew you and they gave me a pass, as they say in Newark."

"Okay, see y'all later," said Jill.

"Jeez Mikey, what problem did you have with the Space Center?" Steve asked.

Sherri gave Mikey a look that said "Don't do it!' but like some other people, Mikey didn't always listen to his top advisor.

"Well, a couple of Saturdays ago, Sherri and I were selling sea shells at the Farmer's market up the street just past the 7 Eleven. Sherri had gone across the street to the Ladies Booma when a gigantic wind came up. Everyone was scrambling to hold down their tents and goods for sale when a big gust broke all of the lines that tied our canopy down. So I grabbed four of the lines in desperation and in a flash I was airborne like Mary Poppins and her umbrella".

All the guests started looking at one another with a "this guy is full of it" look.

"Up, up, up I went," Mikey continued. "I barely cleared the telephone wires and the motel roof and was taken right out to the beach. I was heading for the launch pads at the Space Center."

Now the guests knew it was a lie or a story.

"Well, the Space Center picked me up on radar and two drones came flying out to greet me. One had a camera and one had a machine gun and started firing in short bursts. I lost my flip flops and got nicked in the butt, but the worst thing was my tent canopy had a couple of holes in it and I started to spiral down. By the grace of all the angels in heaven I made a three point landing in this mockup of a red Tesla convertible next to the vehicle assembly building."

Melissa was starting to believe him. Steve had

that, sure you did look.

"Immediately I was surrounded by SWAT teams and Special agents of all kinds. All pointing huge automatic attack weapons at me." Mikey took a breath and a gulp of his coffee.

"Then they arrested me for trespass and impersonating Kim Jung Un. Bad haircut."

It was looking bad until one of them must have recognized me and said, 'Hey, aren't you the guy with the blue bucket that picks up trash on the beach? You live near JB."

"That's me," Mikey said and he replied. 'Well, why didn't you say so?"

So they tore up my ticket and drove me back to the Farmer's market. It all happened so fast that Sherri was still asking what happened to me, and when she saw me coming yelled,

"Where's the bleeping tent?" "What happened to your new flip flops" and "How did you get that bloody hole in your butt?"

After they had a little laugh, Sherri said the food was ready and everyone lined up in the kitchen and got a plate. There was the usual turkey and trimmings. Mikey was famous for his turkey, which Sherri listed on the sideboard menu as 'Burkus Turkus.'

"How do you keep the turkey so moist," Don asked.

"Oh, my uncle Marty Ventura, who was a cook all of his life, always invited me to help him. He showed me how to brine meat. That is the secret. My uncle Marty was originally from Italy and would call me 'Don Michaeli', and asked me if I wanted a shot when no one was around to catch us. He was a wonderful man."

Next it was time for presents. Sherri always made sure every guest and Lulu got something. Then it was Mikey's turn to receive his gift. He opened a big nicely wrapped box cautiously to discover...A Bleeping Drone!

It was a beautiful medium blue and had BOOMA hand painted on the side. Inside the box he found some banners to stream behind the drone. One said "Save Our Oceans". Another said, "I Swear because it pleases my

Mother", and the third said "Jesus is not a Bunny".

"The third one is for the Spring Breakers," smiled Sherri.   Sherri never wanted any gifts, so Mikey got them a pair of tickets to the Jimmy Buffet concert that was coming in a few months.

The small talk continued for a few minutes when there was another person looking through the gate. A younger woman who Mikey recognized as the bagger girl from the supermarket seemed to be lost. He greeted her, "Hi, Merry Christmas, can we help you,"

"Hi, my name is Shirley and I am looking for the lady who helps the monkeys. I brought her some bananas," which she proudly held up.

There was a silence until Mikey said, "Can you come in for a moment Shirley? Is anyone with you?"

Shirley cautiously advanced a few feet.

"Shirley, I hate to tell you that Bea passed away a couple of weeks ago, and all of the monkeys have been moved to a zoo for a while."

Shirley's face saddened with the disappointment of a face that had seen a lot of disappointments. There were tears in her eyes.

"Why did she die?" Shirley asked.

"She just fell asleep in her chair watching television while eating some ice cream."

"I've got to go," Shirley said.

"No please, please stay chorused the other guests. We know that Miss Bea would want you to stay..."

Shirley sat down. She looked around at the food and gifts and smiled.

"Have you eaten?" asked Sherri.

"Well, I am going home and I have a frozen turkey dinner. So I can't stay. My mom is out with her boyfriend and she sometimes gets mad at me when I don't let her know where I am. I forget things."

"Let us fix you up a plate to take with you sweetie," said Sherri.

The tears had stopped and Shirley nervously spoke with Melissa and Don. She talked about how much she liked Bea's plan to take care of the monkeys.

"My mother drinks a lot and smokes weed most days," she began. "I think that I'll give her the bananas."

"Great idea," came the unanimous response.

Sherri appeared with two containers of food in a bag. There was a little Christmas card for Shirley that had a twenty slipped in. "Now don't open that card until you get home," she said.

"How will I get your containers back to you?" worried Shirley.

"You just stop by anytime," said Mikey. "Make sure your mom knows where you are. And Merry Christmas."

Shirley smiled a little smile and turned to leave, but when she got to the gate she turned and said, "Thank you. Did you know that Christmas is the Baby Jesus birthday?"

Mikey smiled and now everyone had a tear in

their eye. "Yes we know".

Then she got on her beat up beach bike and started down the sidewalk into another world.

"Merry Christmas Shirley," they all shouted.

Matthew 25:40 *Inasmuch you have done these things to the least of mine you have done it unto me.*

EXPLOSION AT THE DONGLE DANGLER

About two months after Christmas Mikey decided to stop by the VFW to see Charley.

"How's your hammer hangin Mikey",

"Youse talkin' to me?" some things hardly ever change.

After a few minutes Charley took a seat next to Mikey and broke the ice. "Mikey you never told me too much about what happened with your cousin Farticus Burkus except that he had a lot of black haired kids".

"Funny that you should ask Charley, but just a couple of days ago I received an e-mail from that nice girl Meghan Tracey at the Irish Ancestry Society. The Society says that it is rather urgent that I get back to Ireland by the first week in March. It is a little mysterious, but she says it is of great importance, and they are going to pay my plane ticket and my hotel. It is that important."

"Are you going?" Charley asked as excitedly as he could.

"Well, I discussed it with Sherri last night and of course I think she suspects that there might have been some 'friggin'in the riggin' during my last trip. I assured her that there wasn't and she said ok because she needed a break from my blarney.

Charley was pensive, "I wonder about the secrecy?"

"I think it has something to do with the statue of Farticus that was found near Dongle, as well as another statue nearby with the inscription 'Nellie'!!"

So Mikey left for Ireland and a few weeks after St Patrick's Day returned back to finish his tale.

"Well Charley, Sherri still didn't want to go over because of Lulu being sick and so I flew over the second week of March. Meghan Tracey met me at Shannon airport and drove me down to Dongle a small village across the bay from Dingle. It was about two hours and on the way she filled me in on the excitement, which she couldn't say on the Internet because of all the hacking and identity theft.

She told me that a new bath had been found in the ruins of a small castle outside of Dongle. They were certain that it was built by my ancestor Farticus and the locals wanted a genuine descendant of Farticus to assist in the grand opening.   I was it.

We arrived in Dongle just before noon and she got me checked into The Dongle Dangler, a Bed and Breakfast with a good pub and small restaurant. She said she would be back to pick me up at five p.m. sharp."

"I said tanks," because there is no 'th' sound in Gaelic, and everybody says 'tanks','tousands' and 'tree' for three.'

"Okay so I go in and check in with the bartender named Donovan who is really pleasant and gets me into my room which is very nice and has its own booma."

"Nothing but first class for Mikey", poked Charley.

"So then I go downstairs to the bar to get lunch and the place is full and everyone is talkin' until I walk in and then everything gets quiet."   So I say, "Did somebody Fart??" and the whole room goes crazy wild laughing and whistling and everybody is patting me on the back and saying 'Welcome Yank' and the girls are squeezing me and smiling'.   It was a marvelous moment. The bar held about fifty people and had a horse shoe shape with the taps and whiskey at the far end against the wall. It was simply decorated with Irish signs and a few posters, and also had a small platform for a band and a few booths for diners."

"What did the girls look like?" said Charley with a lecherous smile.

"Well, I mean they were mostly in their thirties to fifties and of course very Irish looking, but the barmaid came right up to me and gives me this nice bowl of vegetable and lamb soup. She had long black hair and steel blue eyes and a fantastic figure. Her apron and slacks were black, but she had on a pure white long sleeved peasant's blouse. Her skin was slightly tanned and her only jewelry was a black onyx cross on a thin silver neckless around her neck." Charley's eyes opened wide. "She was just the perfect height, like me".

Then some guy across the bar shouts out, "watch it Farticus , Angelina's a Banshee", to which the barmaid sweetly responds with "Fook off ya impotent vagrant."

Then she turned to me, "Is there anything that I can get ya or help ya with Mister Burkus? My name IS Angelina and I am NOT a Banshee , cause if I were I would turn that vagrant into a newt."

"No tanks Angelina, but you can call me Mikey. Seems everybody knows me."

"Oh, you are going to be quite the hero around here after tonight. We all are counting on you. Make sure you get a good meal and a pint."

"I gave up the grape, so right now I'll have some coffee,"

"Coffee it is," she said with a smile and turned and retreated into the galley."

Then Donovan the bartender says, "I was told by Mayor Brogan himself to give you this package. In it there is a green toga, and he requests that you bring it along or put it on first, but remember it is still pretty cool at night. He will be down to meet you when Meghan picks you up."

"So I said that I would probably wear it over my clothes and he says that would be just fine. The next hour was just full of people asking questions and my relation to Farticus, and what kind of life I led. Stuff like that. They really liked my idea of picking up trash on the beach and taking care of the mermaid."

"Then one rather short man with red hair, short red beard and a twinkle in his eye comes up and introduces himself as Dooley, and then asks if I know why the place is called the Dongle Dangler, which I did not?"

"So Dooley tells me the legend of the place that, at one time, it was reputed to be a vacation spot for nudist leprechauns. They would show up when the weather was getting warm in the beginning of spring or so, and frolic around with their Dongles dangling down, drinking Meade and Potin and having a good craic. Then it seemed the spring that was their bathing spot dried up and they disappeared. And now that we've discovered this ancient bath, they just might return. It would be great for tourism and such."

Charley was transfixed by the story to the point that he needed a beer and Mikey needed a fresh cup of coffee.

"I didn't know the leprechauns used crack!" Charley said.

"No, not crack, the drug.   It is spelled craic in Gaelic means good times, conversation and dancing and such with your friends and comrades.   Like the times we get together and have a good time with the other vets."

"Okay, I gotcha"

"You said that bar maid Angelina might be a Banshee, and I forget what that means," said Charley.

"Well, the Banshee as I understand it, are woman spirits who shriek a God awful scream at night when someone is going to die. It might be like a type of ancient mourners from long times past", Mikey briefly explained.

"Anyway about four o'clock I went to my room to get cleaned up and change. I put on my genuine Irish wool sweater and some jeans and covered them over with the green toga. At just before five Donovan knocked on my door and said that Meghan was here for my ride, and when I opened the door to my room and to my complete amazement, there were five or six men in green togas and wooly green hats who were, with the exception of the Mayor apparently in some state of inebriation, standing ready to escort me. The Mayor, himself, whose name is Peter Brogan greeted me with a hug and shook my hand warmly.

"Tank you, tank you very much Captain Burkus for making this journey. You are a true gentleman. This is a special night. But let us go now and see the bath."

Mikey continued, "We went outside and instead of automobiles there was a line of maybe, I think ten carts drawn by Irish ponies known as Jaunty Carts. All were full of men and women wearing green togas and chanting 'Burkus, Burkus, cut a big one' Burkus, Burkus, cut a big one'. They all had some sort of drink in their hand.

So I got into the lead cart with Mayor Brogan.
Meghan was there too as was the Mayor's
wife Anna, a spirited woman who reminded
me of my housekeeper back in Cocoa Beach.
We started through the paved road to the end
of town, and soon the cooking smells faded
into the sweet grassy fragrances of the
countryside.

After another fifteen minute ride on a gravel
road and in the dimming light we pulled up to
the old castle. It was small as far as castles in
the area go, and not a grand structure
although it might have been in the past. The
walls were all intact, but some of the rocks of
the parapets were in crumbling ruins. The
locals had cleaned up the area around the
castle and it was a nice flat parking area. The
fields around the castle were separated by
gray rock stone walls all the way up the side
of Mount Brandon. Guarding the castle
entrance were the recently uncovered statues
of Farticus Burkus and Nellie Hornius
immortalized as a mermaid.   There were
more people awaiting us who all appeared
very happy in a Guinness and Jamieson sort
of way.

"My kind of people," said Charley.

"Burkus, Burkus, cut a big one..."

But then it became deadly silent when the chilling scream of an unseen Banshee filled the night...

It was so mournful and loud that it sent chills down your spine...until someone in the crowd shouted... "It's that fookin' Angelina but not to worry, let's get on with the fookin' party."

Well Charley, such a cheer arose from that assembly that even a Banshee couldn't stop this party so in we went to the castle.

The entrance room was as you might expect, about one hundred feet across. The ceiling was about thirty feet high which was probably to vent the cooking smoke in ancient times. Medieval sconces and a high hanging chandelier which had been wired for electricity provided the light. A large table was set near a wall and kegs of Guinness and Smithwicks were pouring freely. Angelina was not to be seen. There were no chairs except for three large wooden thrones that were elevated about three feet at the far side room with a huge green and gold curtained banner above them which read, I was told, *The Dongle Danglers Society,* in Gaelic and Latin. On each side of the chairs were large wooden doors which I soon found out led to the bath."

"What happened next?" asked Charley, "were there any leprechauns??"

"A fantastic question," Mikey replied, "not just yet".

In a short while after the initial commotion subsided, Mayor Brogan led me and Meghan to the elevated chairs. He sat in the middle with me on the right and Meghan on the left. Brogan raised his hand and the room became silent...then the Banshee wailed again......in one voice the crowd shouted "Fookin' Angelina"... and then cheered madly.

The Mayor began again. "Mikey Burkus, we thank you for coming here tonight not knowing what was going to be asked of you."

"I raised an eyebrow and felt a bit uneasy. A Secret Society initiation I thought. "

"Tought!!" Charley interjected.

"I stand corrected", smiled Mikey.

The Mayor continued, "In a few minutes we shall all go down through two wooden doors, pointing left and right, to see our recently uncovered Roman Bath built by Farticus Burkus aka Giganticus Padorkus. You were selected to come as a true descendant of Farticus as proven by DNA. Unknown to you until now, Meghan Tracey is a true descendant of his wife Wild Nellie of Mayo. Legend tells us that this is the mythical pool where the leprechauns frolicked, clothes optional..."

A wild cheer erupted from the crowd..."Cut a big one, cut a big one."

The Mayor raised his hand and asked for silence.

"When we found the bath we also found a stone tablet which said that the water was no longer warm and had grown cold. It further stated that a descendant of Farticus Burkus must be found to restart the warm bubbles. That person would receive tree wishes and the love of all the leprechauns."

Then Peter Brogan looked at me with the forceful demanding eyes of a saint, "WILL YOU HONOR THIS LEGEND AND ACCEPT THE CHALLENGE???"

So I tought for a long ten seconds, stood up, smiled and said. "This is a joyful participation in the sorrows of life! What would you have me do?"

The cheering was so loud that the building seemed to shake.

"Weren't you a bit afraid?" asked Charley.

Mikey looked into Charley's eyes and said, "I am a Royal Shellback, since first crossing the Line, the Equator, and have crossed the line many times thereafter survived THAT initiation left me with no fear, as certified by King Neptune himself to all slimy pollywogs."

Charley was speechless but smiling.

Mikey continued his tale.

The Mayor spoke.

"First knowing that you like me, no longer

drink alcohol, we cannot ask you to drink meade or potin. In its place we have a special liquid concoction that will generate a little gaseous stimulation in your innards. Then while the assembled crowd observes, you must descend into the pool, sit on the bottom and...Fart... as Farticus of old. The bubbles must rise to the surface emitting a BURKUS as proof of your accomplishment... ARE YOU READY????"

"What did you say?" asked Charley.

"BRING IT ON AND FOOK ANGELINA!!!

"So I was led through the right door with all of the dignitaries which descended into the side of the bath. The crowd went through the left door which led to a small tiered amphitheater which afforded all to see the ceremony, even if a bit crowded.

The bath was square and about sixty feet on each side. It was perhaps three to four feet deep. It was beautifully made of polished marble, and inscribed into the wall in the middle of the bath was chiseled "Farticus Burkus" and so I realized that it was true, this was a genuine Farticus Burkus bath. The water was the clearest that one could imagine. I took off my shoes and socks then dipped in my now naked toe. It was pretty cold, perhaps sixty degrees Fahrenheit.

I thought, I am going to have to take my sweater and pants off to do this. So I pulled up my toga and stripped them off, leaving me in my U S Navy style white boxers. What to do? So I put my toga back on and descended the stairs, then took off my boxers.

As I slowly eased myself in to the cold water I discovered that the toga was see through material when wet. Women gasped, "My Gawd".

A man yelled, "I thought that Saint Patrick had driven out all of the snakes!"

Another "Giganticus Padorkus"!

Yet another, "Don't let the White House know about that padorkus"!

As I further lowered myself the mayor's liquid concoction began to react and create a gaseous internal reaction. I was getting ready to cut the cheese.

Squatting to begin my task, the crowd began a low chant "no poopus, no poopus, no poopus.."

I had to steady myself with one end of the pool as I fully squatted feeling the cold marble below...it was really cold now...the Banshee screamed....   "Fook Angelina" roared the crowd, and then Mayor Brogan's concoction began to well up in my intestine, and suddenly there was a BOOM !! But was it a BAAAARROOM or a BOOMA??? The water felt suddenly warm.. OH NO..."no poopus, no poopus..." but when I looked down THE WATER WAS PERFECTLY CLEAR and a great bubble surfaced, BURKUS EXPLOSIVUS!

Warm bubbles now began to surface like a large fish tank...THE PUMP HAD BEEN PRIMED...THE BANSHEE STOPPED WAILING, A GLORIOUS DAY. THE BATH HAD COME TO LIFE"!!!

There were loud reverberations off the wall and water as the crown roared "FARTICUS BURKUS NO POOPUS, FARTICUS BURKUS NO POOPUS!!"

Then Mayor Brogan and a couple of other strong men helped lift me from the bath and gave me a towel to dry off and reclaim my clothes. The crowd was jumping or falling into the pool. An older woman posted a sign "NO Diving This End." I found out later that she once was a nun and was now a condo commando.

After about twenty minutes of bedlam, most returned to the upper castle chamber. We again mounted the little platform and stood next to the small thrones. Then we were joined by that fellow Dooley, the one at the bar with the red hair.

The mayor quieted the crowd and Dooley read from what appeared to be an ancient scroll:

"This is to certify to all present and whosoever have the need of this knowledge, that on this day, Saint Patrick's Day, March 17th, 2018 AD that Mikey Burkus ancestor of Farticus Burkus and Nellie of Mayo, became a Knight of the Dongle Danglers, and deserving of all the honors and respect of the title." signed Dooley O'Reilly Royal

Leprechaun.

So then there were hugs and handshakes all around and I made a short speech and finally asked the crowd, "What was in that concoction?" to which the Mayor replied.

"We got it on the Internet from Farticus Motors, it's called Liquid Beano and Prune Juice or BeanoPrun."

"Now the Mayor announced that I must make three wishes. That was tough one. So I used that old trick that my sweet mother Kathleen taught me, "Follow your heart.""

"And then I taught of Saint Teresa"...

"Live your Heaven by doing good on Earth"

So I cleared my throat and said:

First...   World Peace

Second…   The End of Want

Turd...   The End of Ignorance and Prejudice

"Are you sure that is what your wishes are Farticus?" asked Dooley O'Reilly. "Leprechauns can't grant miracles.   But we all can try can't we"

"That's it, there's nothing else that could top tonight's festivities", I smiled.

"Wow", Charley said in a low voice. "I would have wished for..."

"Oh, I have a good idea of what you might have wished for, but then you might die of exhaustion in two weeks. Or a Banshee might turn you into a newt. Gotta run Charley, the mermaid needs breakfast," said Mikey.

REFLECTIONS

Two days later Meghan picked up Mikey to return home. As they rode to Shannon Airport, Mikey asked? "Why did the Banshee wail that night?"

Meghan paused and took a deep breath, " Might have been for you and it might have been for me, and it might have been for who knows?"

"We think that when Farticus died, Nellie couldn't live with the humans any longer. She recovered her mermaid skin from its long used secret hiding place, and summoned all of the children and grandchildren to her cottage by the sea. They were startled by her appearance and began to cry and say, "No, no, you must not leave us and when will we ever see you again." She comforted them and said she would be resting a while in the silent mind of the Power until they would all be together again. She reminded them that to many people, the message of the cross is that 'there must be a death to be a resurrection and there were many forms of death, not only of a loved one, but the death of a marriage in divorce, the death of your mind by booze and drugs, the loss of a limb by accident or in the field of battle. But for all of these things there can be a resurrection, or we can let ourselves fall into a rut of self-pity. Then she finished by saying that the only difference between a rut and a grave is the size."

Meghan continued, "they helped her to the beach and she dove into the sea and disappeared."

Mikey said, "Meghan, how do you know this?"

She replied, "It came to me in a dream not so long ago. It was as if Nellie wanted me to know? Do you believe me?"

"How could I not believe you? You are my only cousin who is a mermaid."

Meghan dodged a few sheep and waved to the shepherd. "That's Dingus," she said.

Mikey nodded, "You know Meghan I noticed as we were leaving Dongle this morning that there's a group of solar panels on the roof of the castle. Hard to see them at night. Are they powerful enough for the lights?"

"Ah, yes," smiled Meghan again, and then quietly murmured, "and for some other tings too,"

"Oh, what other tings?"

"I taught you woulda guessed, Mikey. The other tings are the bubbling warm water pump!! Did I just burst YOUR bubble??"

They both laughed until tears rolled down their cheeks.

"And will there be an admission?" asked Mikey

"Ten euros admission and five for a picture when bathing in the soothing waters of "Dongling Warm Bubbling Springs"!!

The good news was that the Society of Dongle Danglers had voted to establish a fund for Mikey Burkus and that he would receive one per cent of the annual net earnings of Dongling Warm Bubbling Springs in addition to a lifetime free admission to the baths in exchange for an annual appearance at a time to be later agreed upon.

This was great news and Mikey started

thinking immediately on how to provide a college education for his granddaughter Zoe in the event of his sudden demise.

"Well, tanks Meghan for everyting. It was a fantastic time."

"We shall never forget you Farticus Burkus, your name is carved into the wall." and then she was gone and soon his plane was passing over the spectacular Cliffs of Moher that bordered the Atlantic, the last parish before America. Mikey settled in for the long flight. The first class seat was more than he had even hoped for. Great food and free booze if he had chosen, which he did not.

It had been a long week of an exceptional experiences. He was not interested in the movie offerings and spent the first few minutes paging through an Irish magazine. As he gazed out the window into the now darkening clouds, he started to think about his life. This had been one of the best things that had happened. A true unexpected gift.

Sadly, it brought to mind the mistakes he had made in the near and distant past. No matter how he cut it, his major failures for the most part reflected in his boozing. It had deadened his marriages, alienated his children, and resulted in missed opportunities to prosper or do more than he might have. Although he was brought up at a time that booze was glorified as it was in the life pursuits that he had chosen, he had until the comparatively recent years, been a hard drinker.

Through some miracle he enjoyed excellent health. The tours in Vietnam, involvement in three other wars, multiple dangerous exploits on and off the sea, running the alleys of exotic and some not so exotic cities of the world. The people, the food, the faces, the smells. Just surviving difficult situations brought on by people who, for one reason or another, just didn't like him.

"Maybe it was my humor," he speculated.

If he had to do over he would have given up the adventures for more time with his kids. He rarely saw or even heard from them anymore. They were separated by so many miles and understandably lived their own lives with their own families.

" ...for of all sad words of tongue or pen,

the saddest are these,.,'It might have been…"[1]

Now after all of the wins, losses, medals, accolades and criticism he would be immortalized for farting in a bath tub.   Go figure!

BEYOND THE SOMBRERO GALAXY

Not too long after Mikey returned from Dongle, there was a memorial for Bea at the Community Church near the beach. Mikey had been to several memorial services in the past fifteen years. Coming from the formality of his upbringing and his years as a naval officer he was at first surprised by the informality of Cocoa Beach services. Bea's family came down from Maine, members of the condo community and her church assembled in a little flowered garden to spread her ashes in the place that she loved. Mikey poured a small glass of red wine on the ground when no one was looking.

After Bea's memorial things got back to their routine. The beach had begun the slow process of repairing itself but it would take a major rehabilitation requiring millions of dollars to return the sand. There were still plenty of beach goers at low tide, but high tide now came all the way to the dunes, and also brought strong rip tides making it dangerous especially for the younger kids. Mikey's daily routine now was oriented to the

tides, following behind the high tide to gather the debris entangled with the seaweed.
Human snow birds now began to return. Their presence was made known by increased street traffic, out of state license plates and beeping of horns. The other sign was cigarette butts both on the streets and on the beach.

One morning while starting his rounds on Slater Way, an extremely attractive young woman quietly pulled up alongside him on her beach bike cruiser. The bike's fenders were a shiny red with flames added for accent.

Her rather fantastic body was clad in a very revealing bikini and she smiled the sweetest of smiles.

"Don't you just hate people?" she asked.

"Not really," replied Mikey," but I do get disappointed."

"How much do they pay you for picking up trash? Maybe I can get a job."

"I work for my wife who is a mermaid. She won't make me breakfast and makes me sleep on the couch if I don't keep the beach clean."

"What are you anyway, some kind of Wise Guy?"

"I used to be, but I gave it up, I'm a retired Wise Guy sort of New Joisey,"

The woman maneuvered her bike a bit closer. "My name is Lucy, what's yours sailor? How would you like to get real, I mean real lucky?"

"What did you have in mind?" said Mikey as memories of his younger days slowly crept into his head, not to mention his beach shorts.

"Well, I always appreciated a slightly older gentleman such as you, and thought perhaps we could go behind that big sand dune and get to know each other, a LOT better."

"Lucy, I am very tempted, but was there something else on your mind?'

"Well sailor, you got a twenty I could hold. You may not have another chance like this ever," she said, bending over to show a better view of her physical charms.

Mikey remembered the guidance from a Kipling poem,

"...and the sins that you do by two and two you shall pay for one by one..."[2]

He closed his eyes and took a deep breath.

"Lucy, I'm sorry but I'll have to turn you down," he said apologetically. "I'm out of Viagra."

Lucy's smiling face became almost magically changed into one of anger and rage. "You stupid old man, this was maybe your last chance for a good time. Go back to being a garbage man," and with that she wheeled around and quickly peddled away revealing a little devil with a pitchfork tattooed on her right buttocks. Mikey watched her fade down the street thinking about past missed chances.

The encounter had unusually tired him. After the long trip back from Key Largo, the adventure in Dongle, the rigors and sadness of Bea's passing, Lulu's illness, he suddenly felt very old.   As he turned toward the water he became aware of an unusually bright white light on the sand. At first he thought that it might be a bride posing for her nuptials, but then it faded away. "Strange", Mikey thought as he continued heading towards the water.

He picked out a larger sand dune not far from the tide line and sat down. He checked around to make sure that lovely Lucy wasn't ready to pounce.

The morning air and sea were particularly beautiful with a pretty good break for the surfers and paddle boarders who were catching some decent rides and heading back out again. He broke out his coffee mug and unscrewed the top. Still warm.

Up the coast he could see a large container ship followed by a tug and barge offshore. They apparently were waiting for a big cruise ship to clear the port on its way to the Bahamas or Caribbean. The ships brought back memories of all his years at sea and all of the places he had visited, and the storms, and the music and the people and he closed his eyes and fell into a deep sleep. It was his deepest sleep ever. In his dream he again saw the brilliant white light. There was a figure in the light, and as the light faded he could make out the figure of a tall bare breasted woman with long flowing black hair sitting only a few feet in front of him. The name Nellie was tattooed over her heart. She had brown skin, and to his amazement he realized that it was a mermaid. Not just any mermaid. It was, THE MERMAID.

She spoke. "Michael. Welcome. I've been looking for you. Have you picked up any trash today?"

Mikey cleared the light halos from his eyes. "Why not yet, I just got started, but I was interrupted,"

"Oh," said the mermaid, "I was watching the whole thing. That was Lucy trying to tempt you," she said with an Irish lilt. "Her real name is Lucifer I am told. Come on and I'll make you some breakfast if you've got a pretty shell for me."

Mikey stood up in dumbfounded silence. "Of course I have a very special shell for you", and pulled out a golden scallop from his net bag. "Why did you call me Michael?"

"Well, that is your name isn't it, and your mother told me to call you Michael if I ever ran into you."

"My mother?" He paused, "And when did you see her? She died almost fifty years ago." And then he realized her mission," Is it time? Is it my time to go?"

The mermaid smiled and stretched out her flipper and raised herself partially from the sand. "You'll be able to understand all about it in a very short time, no worries," and smiled a most reassuring smile.

"Then I was right."

"You were right Michael, and just call me Nellie."

"Are you related to the Nellie in my stories?"

"I AM the Nellie in your stories."

"Why aren't the other beach goers staring at us," he asked.

"They can't see me, and soon they will not see us!"

"What happens next Nellie? Where are we going?"

The mermaid straightened and elevated herself to an astounding height of ten feet tall. The seagulls flew silently above her head, and the morning sun in her hair made the small shells trapped there glisten like precious jewels. Her scent was sweet but musky and her voice now sounded like a far off gentle song.

She opened her arms and took Mikey in a heavenly embrace, and he knew that he mattered and that he always mattered, and that he was loved and had always been loved, and that he was safe.

She spoke. "And now we will travel across this unmeasurable universe to a place beyond the Sombrero Galaxy, and rest a while in the peaceful and silent mind of the Power until another voyage comes along or perhaps for all eternity."

"I'm ready," he replied. "How will we get there?"

Nellie smiled, "Swim of course. Use the breast stroke."

And she inhaled his soul into hers and gently lowered his now expired human body to the sand. Then in one spectacular motion sprung a mighty dive into the sea and disappeared, taking them on his final eternal journey.

That was how they found Mikey Burkus, as if sleeping peacefully on the sand dune looking out to sea. In his hand was a half full coffee mug decorated with the likeness of a beautiful mermaid and a solid gold scallop shell in his pocket.